Bittersweet Journey

Books by Carrie Bender

Willowcreek Series

1. *Willowcreek Valley Farm*
2. *Bittersweet Journey*

Whispering Brook Series

3. *Whispering Brook Farm*
4. *Summerville Days*
5. *Chestnut Ridge Acres*
6. *Hemlock Hill Hideaway*
7. *Woodland Dell's Secret*
8. *Timberlane Cove*

Miriam's Journal

1. *A Fruitful Vine*
2. *A Winding Path*
3. *A Joyous Heart*
4. *A Treasured Friendship*
5. *A Golden Sunbeam*
    Miriam's Cookbook

Dora's Diary

1. *Birch Hollow Schoolmarm*
2. *Lilac Blossom Time*
3. *Beyond Mist-Blue Mountains*

WILLOWCREEK SERIES ②

Bittersweet Journey

Carrie Bender

A. B. PUBLISHING
Ithaca, Michigan

Publication Data

Bender, Carrie
Bittersweet Journey / Carrie Bender.
    p. cm.— (Willowcreek series ; 2)

Summary: Steven and Annie, a young Amish couple in Tennessee, read and discuss an epic story about Mennonites migrating from Pennsylvania to Upper Canada (Ontario) two hundred years ago.

    [1. Amish and Mennonites— Fiction. 2. Farm life— Fiction.
3. Family life— Fiction.] I. Title. II Series: Bender, Carrie.

Willowcreek series ; 2

The story of Sam Bricker and Beccy Eby is adapted from *The Trail of the Conestoga* (1924/25), by B. Mabel Dunham, by permission of the Aden Eby family, who holds the rights to the book. This work of fiction is true to Mennonite life. Various historical resources report on the land purchase and migration, such as "Ontario," in *The Mennonite Encyclopedia;* and chap. 13 in John L. Ruth, *The Earth Is the Lord's.*

Pennsylvania German words are explained and spelled in accord with C. Richard Beam's *Revised Pennsylvania German Dictionary* (Brookshire Publications, 1991). Scripture is adapted from the King James Version.

BITTERSWEET JOURNEY
Copyright © 2003 by the Author. All rights reserved
International Standard Book Number: 1-881545-32-6
Printed in the United States of America
Published by A. B. Publishing, 3039 S. Bagley Rd., Ithaca, MI 48847
Cover art by Julie Martin
Inside illustrations by Julie Martin, and David Nolt (on p. 73), and
    from B. Mabel Dunham's *Trail of the Conestoga* (on pp. 6 and 144)
Book design by Garber Editing, 300 S. High St., Scottdale, PA 15683

12 11 10 09 08 07 06 05 04 03   10 9 8 7 6 5 4 3 2 1

To order, please contact A. B. Publishing (at address shown above):
    Phone: 1-800-882-6443   Fax: 1-800-645-8079
    E-mail: abpub@abpub.com   Web site: www.abpub.com

Contents

1

A Rainy Day

Annie Petersheim stood at the kitchen window watching the icy rain pouring down in sheets. It was splashing against the windowpane and washing in rivulets off the porch roof and into the spouting, then cascading into the rainwater barrel at the corner of the washhouse.

"Back home in Summerville, this fall moisture would probably be in the form of snow," she mused aloud, thinking wistfully of the sledding and skating parties of bygone winters. "I know we need the rain to raise the water table before the ground freezes, but it sure makes for a dreary day."

Much as Annie had learned to like it in Willowcreek Valley with her husband, Steven, there were still times when her thoughts traveled back to her girlhood home, with wistful memories of her carefree youth. The wind rattled at the windowpanes, and Annie turned away, glad that not many days were as stormy as this one.

She went to the woodbox and selected a good-sized piece of firewood. Lifting the round lid of the big black Columbian range, she shoved it into the fire, sending up a shower of sparks. The stove, which served double duty for heating and cooking, glowed rosy red, filling the old-fashioned kitchen with warmth and cheer.

"Time to get back to my quilt," Annie murmured, eyeing her sore, needle-jabbed fingers a bit ruefully.

"But I'm tired of quilting, and I'd rather be . . . I'd like nothing better right now than going for a long walk, back to the *Buschland* (woods) and the lake. I haven't been there for ages, it seems.

"Better yet, I could go to see Dan Vernie (Dan's wife, Vernie); she always manages to cheer me up. But I know I can't do that in this rain, since Rusty is not a woman's horse. Hmmm, I seem to have a rather bad case of cabin fever. Oh, well, Steven and neighbor Dan will be back from the horse sale after awhile, and then— "

Annie's thoughts were cut short by the clatter of wheels and hoofbeats in the driveway. With an exclamation of joy she flew back to the window and saw a familiar bay horse and *Dachweggli* (roofed buggy) coming in the drive at a brisk trot. "It's Vernie, driving alone!" she cried happily. "That means she can likely spend the afternoon here. *Wunderbaar!*"

Vernie guided her horse under the forebay (overhang) of the barn, tied him, then took her umbrella out of the *Weggeli* and came splashing to the house. Annie threw open the door and happily ushered Vernie inside.

"I see your quilt's not out of the frame yet," Vernie said as she unpinned her shawl. "I came to help, if you don't mind. I knew you'd return the favor after the quilt I'm piecing is in the frame."

"Mind!" Annie exclaimed. "You can't imagine how delighted I am. It sure seems lonely around here when Steven's not home. I don't know how I'd manage without my good neighbor, Dan Vernie."

Vernie laughed. "Nor I, without my Steve Annie. We'd better get together as often as we can this winter, because next summer we'll both be a lot more tied down." She took her thimble out of her pocket and seated herself at the quilt.

"What a beautiful blending of colors," she marveled. "I've always liked the tumbling block pattern, and this dusty blue and rose color combination brings out the design even more. It puts to shame my lowly flower garden quilt in peach and green. I wish I'd have your knack of knowing what goes nice together."

"Pure flattery." Annie brushed off the compliment with a smile. "You are the one who has the knack." The two young housewives' tongues flew faster than their needles, for they were best friends and had a lot in common. The subjects ranged from new recipes, quilt patterns, babies, and husbands, to healthy neighborhood gossip. The afternoon flew by as if on wings.

"Are Dannie and the lively little Erika coming again next spring?" Vernie asked. "I remember Dannie saying he hoped to be your *Gnecht* (hired man) next summer, but he wasn't sure."

"Dannie will likely come," Annie replied. "We've asked Steven's sister Susie to come, too, but we haven't heard from her yet. Perhaps she's promised elsewhere. But Erika's not coming; she's going to spend the summer with her mother in Florida, I believe. I must admit that, lovable as she was, I'm rather relieved that she didn't ask to spend the summer with us here in Willowcreek Valley again. She's quite a handful."

"Angelic little wildcat," Vernie chuckled. "I was just going to say that we'll probably have a few more nests of kittens for her, if she's coming."

Later, as Vernie glanced out the window, she suddenly pushed back her chair and jumped up from the quilt. "Oh, my, it's starting to get dark already, and I must hurry home to put on supper. How can the time have flown so?"

"Stay here for supper," Annie urged. "Dan will know where you are, and he can come for supper, too."

Vernie shook her head. "Not this time. I have stuffed pig stomach slow-roasting in the gas oven, so supper should be ready when I get home.

"Oh, I nearly forgot: I brought a few books along for you to read." She pulled out a plastic bag from under her shawl and handed it to Annie. "Maybe you've read them before. The one is *Hidden Rainbow*, by Christmas Carol Kauffman, a really good book, and— "

"I've read that one," Annie interrupted. "But that was years ago when I was in school, and I'd like to read it again. What's the other one?"

Vernie got it out of the bag and showed it to Annie. "It's the story of a group of Mennonites who started a new settlement in Ontario, Canada, in the early 1800s. Parts of it are in journal form."

Annie paged through the book. "Then it's a true story?"

Vernie nodded. "It was based on the book *The Trail of the Conestoga*. As in all tales from history, the author adds thoughts, feelings, and conversations. That makes it so interesting.

"The main characters, Beccy Eby and Sam Bricker, are real people who lived about two hundred years ago and migrated from Brickerville, Pennsylvania, to Ontario, in Conestoga wagons. The story has been handed down from generation to generation. The author of *The Trail of the Conestoga* was Mabel Dunham, a relative of the Brickers."

"It sounds interesting," Annie said. "It will give me something else to do besides quilting all the time, when my housework is finished. Steven and I will probably read it together in the evenings."

After Vernie had gone, Annie leafed through Vernie's books for awhile, then she eyed the clock and quickly began to prepare supper. She peeled potatoes and fetched a can of stew meat from the pantry, still left there from butchering day, and put it on the range to fry and make gravy.

Then she hurried to the cellar for a jar of peaches, a quart of canned corn, and a head of endive stored there from her fall garden, to make a salad. Glancing out to the barn, she saw that Steven was home, unhitching Lady, the mare they had bought to hitch double with Rusty on far trips and to use as a spare horse.

She hurried with the supper preparations, eagerly looking forward to reading Vernie's books after the supper dishes were washed. Annie glanced at the half-finished quilt with a twinge of guilt, but then told herself, "Oh, well, my fingers really are sore from jabbing them with my needle, and they deserve a rest. I've been quilting all day, and 'all work and no play' wouldn't be good either. So I'll enjoy a relaxing evening of reading. Steven deserves a break, too."

2

Sam and the Schimmel

After supper was over and the barn chores were done, Annie and Steven walked to the house together. The stars were twinkling in the dusty skies overhead, and a blustery wind had sprung up.

"It's cleared off," Steven observed. "I suppose we're in for some cold weather now."

"Brrr!" Annie pulled her chore coat tightly around herself and quickened her step. It would be good to get back to the warm kitchen, and Vernie's books seemed to be beckoning to her.

"I'll make some popcorn," Steven offered, "and then we can find out if those books of Vernie's are worth anything."

Annie nodded. "Let's read them together, side by side on the settee."

Steven chuckled. "Sounds romantic, but no thanks. You can read so much faster than I. If you don't mind, I'll read *Hidden Rainbow*, and you can have the other one. I like to read at my own pace." He took the corn popper out of the pantry and set it over the hot stove lid, then poured in the yellow kernels.

"All right," Annie agreed. "But I can't wait to start reading until you're done popping corn. First I'll just run to the cellar for some apples."

She reached up to get the big fruit bowl out of the cupboard, grabbed a flashlight, and skipped down the stairs. *Those big Rome beauties will go well with the popcorn,* she thought. She quickly washed the apples, selected a juicy one, and then curled up on the big Boston rocker and began to read.

The first journal entry began:

December 19, 1792—Brickerville, Pennsylvania. I, Beccy Eby, take my new journal and pen in hand, to jot down my thoughts, on this nineteenth day of December in 1792. My thirteenth birthday was on Monday, and dear Uncle Christian was well-meaning enough to think of me on his trip to Lancaster that day. He came home with a parcel (this journal) for me, and a few kind words along with it. Aunt Nancy sniffed her disapproval. She doesn't hold much for journal writing, but I didn't care.

It's been three weeks now since I came to live here in this big Hammer Creek House, with Uncle Christian, Aunt Nancy, cousins Susie, Hannes, *der glee Bench* (Little Benj), as they call him, and little Lizzie, and the others. Peter, the oldest son of the family and an ordained preacher, is married and lives nearby. Auntie has a rather sharp tongue sometimes, but underneath, I suspect, she has a heart of gold and kindness. She is very industrious.

Hammer Creek House is quite big and respectable. It stands on the summit of a hill overlooking the Brickerville Road, and it's called after the stream that flows through the meadow, the Hammer Creek. To me, it seems like a real mansion: two stories high and built of clean gray sandstone, sporting spacious windows with many small panes of glass. At the windows are homespun white linen blinds, adjusted with great precision. The front door is made of heavy oak, and above it there is a rectangular slab of red sandstone on which is carved:

John and Elizabeth Eby

1754

Gott gesegne dieses Haus
Und alle was da gehet ein und aus;
Gott gesegne alle sammelt,
Und dazu das ganz Land.

(May God bless this house
and all who here go in and out;
God bless all who gather here,
And also this whole country.)

Yes, it's a grand old house, and a good place to gather for church services. But oh, how I would prefer to live yet on the dear old farm in the backwoods, in the little log house with all my family. We were so happy, all together, Mama, Papa, and our whole family, before . . . before my father, Jeremiah Eby, died of consumption this fall. I can't bear to write about it yet without crying. We all clung to each other—that is, until the day of the sale in November. It was another sad day for our bereaved family, a day of separation and heartbreak.

All our farm stock and household goods were sold, but still there was nothing left over but debts. Mama, in poverty, had to parcel all us children out to relatives and move back home to *Grossdaadis* (grandparents, Mama's parents). Only my older brother Daniel will remain on the farm, but as a hired hand to

15

work for the new owner. It's a terrible thing to have our family thus scattered, but I guess I'm lucky to have Uncle Christian and Aunt Nancy as foster parents, and to be able to live in this stately Hammer Creek mansion.

Uncle is well-known for his good judgment and large-heartedness. His reputation for piety and hospitality grows with each passing year. For a long while already, this house has also been used as a Mennonite meetinghouse on Sundays. It has a huge chimney and an open fireplace in each room, both upstairs and downstairs. Removable partitions of walnut and oak paneling provide a fitting place to come together to worship.

Uncle Christian is a quite kindhearted man, and Auntie means well, too; her bark is indeed worse than her bite. They make me feel welcome and are not lacking in hospitality. I think I shall get along all right here after I get over my *Heemweh* (homesickness), which has been hard to bear. If only . . . *Ya* (yes), well, I must lay this aside and go to help Susie with the milking.

It's chilly here in my little cubicle off the spare room. I could have slept with Susie in the big bedroom, where it's nice and warm, but I'd rather have this hideout of my own. Now der glee Bench is calling me, so I must go.

✍

January 6, 1793, Sunday—Today's weather was quite cold, snowy, and blustery. The wind drove the snow into every nook and cranny, and deeply covered the road leading past here from Brickerville to Lititz. Overnight every old eyesore, stump, and bramble thicket was transformed into a thing of shimmering beauty, a marvelous sight indeed.

In the morning we wondered whether anyone would be able to come to meeting, with the roads drifted over with snow and blocked at low places. But preparations were made, fires were kindled in the large front rooms, and Little Benj was running about here and there, arranging benches and chairs. The Bible and hymnbooks were placed on the leaders' table, and all was in readiness a whole hour before the time set for the meeting. Little Benj stood at the window, watching for the first arrival, bolstering his faith with hope.

Auntie declared that no one would be able to come, and besides, if any of the neighbors would make it through the snow, who would do the preaching? After all, her preacher son, Peter, was sick. Susie suggested a substitute preacher, but Auntie shook her head. No one could preach like Peter. "He's such an earnest, forceful speaker, and a very devout man," she said. "Put the chairs back against the wall again, Benj," she instructed. "No one will be able to come."

The words were scarcely out of her mouth when Uncle Christian made the joyful announcement that someone was coming up the lane—a rider on horseback.

We all went to the window. "It's Sam Bricker," der glee Bench cried, dancing around in high glee. Apparently Sam is a favorite of his, and he was happy at the prospect of having a romp with his hero.

"Just look once! He's riding a *Schimmel* (white horse with small black specks)," Hannes exclaimed. "Looks like a good horse, even if he's white."

I peered out the frosty window and saw a stalwart youth dismounting. The most noticeable thing about him was his curly red hair showing from under his black hat. And then my heart felt like it skipped a beat when I took a second look at the horse. It was a *Schimmel*, and there was a familiar look about him. It was none other than my own dear *Schimmel*, my Menno!

A great lump was gagging my throat as I turned away from the window and huddled in the corner, sitting on the woodbox behind the stove and choking back sobs. Menno would never be mine again. The Brickers had bought him at the auction sale. They had paid twenty dollars for him, and so he was lost to me forever.

Oh, how I had loved to ride him back through our meadow lane, wild and free, my *schtruwwlich* (uncombed) hair flying in the wind. I had named him Menno—after Menno Simons, the early leader in our Mennonite faith. My older brother Daniel had found me crying at the sale when the Brickers were bidding on the *Schimmel*, and he scolded me for being such a *Heilboppeli* (crybaby). "Menno was far from perfect, you know. Why, once he even kicked the dashboard out of the buggy. You'll just have to get over your foolishness."

17

And so I had—until now. When I saw my horse at the Hammer Creek House, it all came back to me, and the tears flowed. Uncle Christian noticed that I had left the window and asked if I had recognized the colt, but I was too choked up to answer, so I retreated to the woodbox. Aunt Nancy drew up a chair beside me and with unusual tenderness stroked my hair and asked, "What's the matter?"

This sympathy from my undemonstrative aunt was so unexpected that I burst into tears and sobbed aloud. Between gasps, I managed to say that I wished I could go back home, and that Menno could be my own horse again.

She shook her head. "You can't do that," she said matter-of-factly. "Your papa went, and he left nothing behind but debts. You're fortunate to have a home with us. This is a much better home than your little log house way back there in the *Busch* (woods)."

This brought a fresh flood of tears from my eyes. After all, to us it was "home, sweet home." We were happy together there. My aunt had meant her words for good, but they cut to the quick. Into an open wound she had poured acid, mistaking it for soothing oil.

Auntie lost all patience then and said severely, "Rebecca Eby, you ought to be ashamed of yourself for acting so *kindisch* (childish). Stop it now and come along out to see the horse." As she left, I heard her muttering something about "*dumm* (dumb) notions, just like all the other Ebys."

In utter dejection I sat there in the corner on the woodbox, until Uncle Christian came over to me and patted me on the head. "Come to the window once, Beccy," he whispered. "You'll want to meet Sam, too. He's in our *Freindschaft* (circle of relatives) yet, just like you are, but from the Bricker side instead of the Ebys. He's got red hair, Sam has, curly red hair, and he's real smart. Everybody likes him."

But I shook my head no. "I don't want to meet Sam at all. He took my dear horse from me. I hate him," I cried between sobs, in a bitter tone of voice.

Uncle Christian stood back, aghast. It was against his pious Mennonite soul to hate anything but the world, the flesh, and the devil. "Oh, come now, Beccy," he begged, "it can't be that bad.

If you don't want to meet Sam, we'll wait till he's in the house. Then you and I will slip out through the front door to the barn, where we can see the *Schimmel* undisturbed by the presence of the horse's new master. Surely you want to greet your horse once more."

How kind of Uncle Christian! We donned our coats and boots and headed for the barn, unnoticed by the others, or so I thought. I was joyously stroking the *Schimmel's* face, head, and ears, and telling him that I loved him, and that he was my own Menno, when the barn door opened. There stood the hated Sam Bricker, gazing at me with a kindly look in his eyes and a smile on his face. I tried to bolt for the door, but Uncle Christian stopped me.

"You don't have to make strange, Beccy," he said. "It's only Sam, and he comes here often."

I shyly turned around to face him. He held my small hand in his large one and told me, "I'll often be coming here to the Ebys, and Menno will come along every time. For as long as I'm here, Menno is yours."

All my hatred vanished instantly, and soon I was smiling through my tears, looking into his laughing eyes. I knew that Sam and Menno were going to be my good friends—the best.

So it was a good Sunday for me after all, even though hardly anyone showed up for the meeting on account of the snow. Before he left, Sam whispered to me that the next time he came, if the roads were not too deep with snow, he would take me for a ride in Uncle Christian's cutter (sleigh), with Menno hitched to it, and that he would let me drive.

Now I'm sorry that I said I hated Sam. Things have turned around so much that I like him a lot. Little Lizzie is calling me for supper, so I must stop scribbling. But I'll add yet that I'm feeling happier than I ever did since coming to the Hammer Creek House, and it's all because of Sam Bricker and Menno visiting here.

O

The clock on the mantle was striking nine, and Annie reluctantly placed a marker in her book, got out of the rocker, and stretched herself. It was time to bank the fire for the night, so she stuffed some more wood into the range and cut the draft back.

Steven was still engrossed in his book. *It must be a good one*, she thought, and was about to say so when she noticed that his head was nodding. The book was sliding forward and was about to fall to the floor. She rescued it and gently tweaked his ear to awaken him. It was time for bed now, but tomorrow night there would likely be more time for reading.

3

The Canada Bug

For the next few days, Annie was busily canning pears—Keiffer pears, the kind that are picked in the fall and put into storage to ripen until colder weather comes. Her days were so full that she wasn't able to put any stitches into her quilt at all until after the supper dishes were washed and the chores done.

So her Beccy Eby book had to be laid aside, and it wasn't till Saturday evening that she had a chance to curl up on the Boston rocker again and read while Steven scanned the farm paper.

Beccy's next journal entry was a month later, in February 1793.

✍

There's an undercurrent of excitement here in the big Hammer Creek House! Uncle Christian seems to have caught the going-to-Canada bug. When he talks about it, a smile hovers over his features, a light sparkles in his eyes, and all of a sudden he seems warm, buoyant, and excited. He seems young again, dreaming dreams and seeing visions in the future.

Auntie calls it "one of his fits" and can be heard muttering, "*Dumm* Eby notions! *Daadi* (daddy) must be in his second childhood!" She rattles her pots and pans in exasperation as she works at the kitchen stove. It must be rather alarming for her.

She keeps a wary eye on him when the first symptoms of the "fit" appear. His face brightens with expectation, and his eyes look steadfastly and unwaveringly into the distance. "Canada" is the magic word that brings a glow to Uncle's kindly old face and brews a storm cloud on Auntie's.

I can't help but wonder what the outcome of it all will be. She is as opposed to the idea as Uncle is for it. It means nothing to her that in Canada there's good, fertile land available for settling on.

Auntie is a domineering woman, and she seems to be worse than ever now that Uncle shows signs of being "feebleminded about going to Canada," as she puts it. This morning after breakfast, Hannes took a book from his pocket and sat down to read. Immediately Auntie was concerned. She bustled over excitedly and looked over her son's shoulder. "Just as I expected: a useless storybook!" she exclaimed to her husband. "He's at it again!"

"*Ach* (oh), leave him be," Uncle said, not in the least alarmed.

Auntie burst out with "That's always the way it is. You let me with all the training to do. All those lies he's reading! It'll ruin him, body and soul!"

Uncle was sufficiently interested in his son's spiritual welfare to put on his spectacles and look over his son's shoulder to see what was the nature of these "lies" Hannes was reading. I peeked, too, and saw the words: "Christian in the Slough of Despond." Uncle, seeing his own name, became absorbed in the story and continued reading, anxious to see if Christian got out of the pit.

With that, Auntie lost her temper and in a huff of righteous indignation cried, "You're reading them lies, too!" She swooped down upon the table, seized the contaminating thing, and threw it into the fire. "There," she said with satisfaction. "Now it can't hurt either of you. Isn't the Bible good enough for you anymore?"

Hannes was amazed at such drastic action but said nothing. He knew it would be no use. I heard Uncle ask him in a whisper, "Where did you get it?"

Hannes whispered back, "From Jacob Brubacher. He got it in Lancaster."

Keeping a watchful eye over Auntie's movements at the fireplace, Uncle drew out his purse, took out several coins, and whispered, "Tell him he can fetch you another one along over when he goes again. But you must hide it, Hannes, or it will land in the fire, too."

Next Little Lizzie was the object of Auntie's domineering. First she chided the child for coming to the table without a covering on her head, as good Mennonite girls are to do. "For shame!" she cried. "Our Lizzie must be a little boy that she sits at the table with a bare head."

Lizzie was quite distressed and hid her face in her kerchief. A little later she was in disgrace again when Auntie's eyes fell upon a great round bread crust that Lizzie thought she had successfully tucked under the edge of her plate.

"Fetch the sulfur, Susie," Auntie commanded. She poured out a big spoonful, mixed it with molasses, and moved it toward Lizzie's pouting little mouth. It was either the crust or the sulfur. But Lizzie sat there, rebellious, refusing to take it until Uncle said, "Crusts give red cheeks, Lizzie, and strong teeth." Then she stuffed the whole crust at once into her mouth.

For a punishment for stalling, Auntie bade her swallow the sulfur mixture, too. When Lizzie drew back and began to cry, Uncle's kind heart was touched, and he said, "Ach, leave her be."

"Leave her be!" Auntie exploded. "That's a sure way of spoiling them!"

"Take it, Lizzie," I whispered in her ear. "I'll wash the dishes if you do." At that, Auntie turned the vials of her wrath on me: "Whatever did you say that for?"

"She'll take it easier if you coax her," I said lamely.

Auntie retaliated, "That's another one of them *dumm* Eby notions. You've all got them, one way or another."

Yes, I really think it's those Canada notions that are making her that way. To her, it's as if someone had gotten an idea to go to the moon and wasn't right in the head. She takes it out on all of us.

Der glee Bench, who is nine, seems to be the apple of his father' eye. He is not a robust child. Like Jacob of old, Uncle seems to love his Benjamin above any of his other sons, and he watches him anxiously least some mischief might befall him.

The other morning, when Auntie had her back turned, I heard him whisper to his son, "Well, Bench, do you feel good today? You must grow big and strong or you can't go along to Canada. You want to go there someday, not?"

And Benj replied, "I'm going along with you."

Of course, Uncle would not think of going without his Benj. In all his visions of journeying to the delectable North, his little son is tramping along in his footsteps. "We must have hope," said Uncle.

"And faith," added Little Benj.

"Yes, and charity too," replied Uncle, who sighed as he glanced at his wife's resolute back. She is his "thorn in the flesh" under the pleasing guise of wife. Yet I know that he would think her wholly satisfactory if only she wouldn't be so opposed to going to Canada.

Eighteen-year-old Susie, too, seems to bear the brunt of Auntie's disapproval. She has a suitor, one named Josiah Schneider. Whenever his name is mentioned, her face is a confusion of blushes, which she tries to hide. But Auntie has no mercy for her daughter's feelings. She claims that Josiah is a lazy, *grossfiehlich* (conceited), *nixnutzich* (good-for-nothing) fellow—plus other failings she is not loath to identify. Auntie has Israel Schantz picked out for Susie and says he would make her a good man. It wonders me what will come of it yet.

Ya, well, I must go and do my chores. Perchance Sam Bricker will come over tonight, on the *Schimmel,* Menno, and give me that promised cutter ride.

○

4

Red Hair at Communion

Beccy's next journal entry is a full seven years later, in 1800. She tries to fill in some gaps of the story.

✒

For a long time I have neglected this journal of mine. As soon as I got over my *Heemweh* here at the Hammer Creek House, I laid it in a drawer and practically forgot about it. Now I am twenty years old, and time has wrought many changes here at my aunt and uncle's house.

Lizzie is a buxom lass in her teens, full of life and color. Der glee Bench is now a young man of sixteen. Suzie is married to

Josiah Schneider. Auntie still disparages him, saying that he will never make a good man for her. I think that is just because Josiah sides with Uncle Christian on this Canada business.

On the matter of the migration to Canada, Auntie is still as adamantly opposed as ever, and Uncle is still as much taken with it. He still takes his Canada "fits" regularly, and she opposes him just as vehemently. It is maddening to think that a freedom-loving soul like Uncle's should be held in such abject bondage to his own wife. She always cows him, and he sinks dejectedly into a chair, with his chin dropped upon his chest. The other day I heard him say to Benj, "If a woman won't, that's all the farther a man gets. But if I were young yet, and not married already—"

"You'd go?" Benj finished for him.

"Yes, I'd go. I hope you will go someday, Bench. I want that someday you will be a preacher in Canada."

Benj hung his head. He did not want to be a preacher, but to please his father, he said, "Maybe."

Some changes have been made in this Hammer Creek House itself over the last seven years. It has been extended to twice its former size, with two front doors instead of one, becoming a double house. In the new part, the *Daadihaus* (grandparents' house), live the *Daadis,* Uncle and Auntie, and the unmarried members of the family. Hannes is married now, and he and his wife and their young ones occupy the older part of the house. He has taken over the responsibilities of the farm.

Yesterday we had communion services here at the Hammer Creek House, which doubles as our meetinghouse. There was a great collection of buggies tied up all around the Eby farm. The service was in charge of the aged bishop, and Uncle and Auntie's oldest son, Preacher Peter, was beside him.

Sam Bricker and Menno were the first to arrive, and he headed straight for the *Daadihaus.* We were still at the breakfast table.

"Ach, but you're early. Did you come to breakfast, maybe?" Benj asked with a laugh. "Come and sit down here beside me." To him, Sam is still the red-headed hero he always was.

So Sam helped himself to a plate from the cupboard, slid in beside Benj, and prepared to enjoy a second breakfast.

"Everything tastes so good here," he said, "pickles and *Schmierkaes* (cottage cheese) and what not all. From how it looks at the table, you must have a pretty good cook."

"Beccy is our cook," Auntie informed him.

This set Lizzie to giggling. "I guess you knew that, Sam. You *yuscht* (just) said that on purpose to see Beccy get red at the cheeks, you teasy boy."

"Teasing—you didn't suck that out of your thumb," Auntie grunted. "That's *yuscht* like them *dumm* Eby notions."

Here Uncle thought it necessary to interrupt. He rather resented the way his wife had of laying all the stupidity she encountered at the door of the Ebys. "Beccy's pretty smart if she gets Sam," he declared.

"That's once you said right," replied Auntie, becoming somewhat agitated. "But she needn't be setting her cap for him. He's took."

At that point, I thought I'd need to leave the table yet, my cheeks burned so to hear them talking about me so.

From across the table, red-headed Sam lifted his eyes from his plate and gazed in amazement at Auntie. "Took, am I? And who do you think took me?"

"Eliza Hoffman," replied Auntie casually. "Her pop says he'll give her the best farm he's got the day she ties up with Sam Bricker."

"But—"

"And I told him he can get the papers ready," continued Auntie, without so much as noticing Sam's attempt to protest. "I said, 'Sam's a Bricker. He's no *Dummkopp* (dunce).'"

Right then, Uncle decided that it was time to change the subject. His eyes were twinkling as if he knew something we didn't. He tilted back his chair to a dangerous angle, tucking his thumbs comfortably into the arms of his waistcoat.

Before long the other worshipers began to arrive, and meeting soon began. I sat beside Eliza Hoffman on the girls' side and wondered if she really was in love with Sam Bricker. I felt a stab of jealously twist in my heart as I thought of her driving with Sam and my Menno, the *Schimmel*.

Mentally, I compared myself with her: No one would have guessed from her dress and appearance that she was the heiress to a valuable *Bauerei* (farm) in the Hammer Creek community. Her snow-white muslin *Kapp* (head covering) was no different from mine, its ribbons not a whit longer. Her dress was cut from the same pattern as the other girls, and her shoes, like ours, were also of cowhide.

When she turned and whispered to me, "Hasn't Sam Bricker got *schee* (beautiful) red hair and such nice brown eyes?" I knew for sure that Eliza was infatuated. I also sensed that it had never entered her silly little head to question whether or not her affection would be reciprocated.

I knew all too well what those soft brown eyes of Sam's could do to me, but I did not think it right to be thinking of such things during the solemnity of communion services, so I did not reply. I was trying to expel from my mind all thoughts of Sam and other things mortal, to center my attention on things divine.

Very devoutly, I buried my face in my hands when we knelt in prayer. But ever and anon, there crept into my thoughts the memory of Sam's little speech at the breakfast table, and there flashed before my eyes the telltale glance that he had shot at me. Did Sam look at Eliza that way, too? Was it just a little, meaningless way he had?

I found my thoughts traveling to what Uncle Christian had said about the Brickers, about Sam and his brother John. Their *Daadi,* Elias, had worked hard to make a living on his farm, but misfortune of one kind or another had dogged him all his life. It had come in the form of a bolt of lightning, destroying his barn and his crops of the season. Then there was a disease that took his fattest beef cattle, and an accident to a valuable cow. Next thing he knew, the bank had failed, and the scant savings of his years had sprouted wings and flown away.

Now only the poor, run-down farm remained. The buildings were small and in urgent need of repair. There was not a less-desirable farm for miles around. His wife, whom he had married to be a helpmeet, was a confirmed invalid, demanding much attention and consideration, not to mention expense.

There were only two sons: the slow and stolid John, who had married Annie; and the red-headed, impulsive Sam. Two sons and only one farm. John as the eldest had inherited the farm, and Sam, for want of something better to do, became a perpetual hired man, without prospects to better himself. He worked hard, pitching sheaves in season and feeding cattle on John's farm, and yet there was no future in it.

I glanced again at Eliza, on the bench beside me. Would Sam fall for her, lured by the prospect of inheriting that good *Bauerei* along with her? He was twenty-six already, and John and Annie felt that it was time for him to get hitched up. I knew they were urging him to take Eliza, but thus far, Sam had dug in his heels.

Just the other day, Annie said to Auntie, "It's time Sam gets married. Eliza Hoffman is soft on him, and she's rich. John's been after him for months, but no, he won't listen. There he sticks, dillydallying, when he has a chance to be running with a girl like Eliza, and her pop has three farms. Sam is, without a doubt, the most popular young man in this community, but stubborn as a mule."

Ach, well, that was just Annie's opinion. I guiltily directed my thoughts back to the sermon. I knew that I must stop thinking about Sam and listen to the bishop. It was happening far too often that even in the middle of a stirring sermon, and when my eyes were supposed to be closed in prayer, that I would find my thoughts straying and catch myself stealing sly glances at Sam. Shame on me! But I feel strangely powerless.

The bishop was vividly portraying the crucifixion of Jesus. Tears were streaming down his cheeks, and his countenance glowed, as with uplifted hands, he pointed the penitent sinner to the foot of the cross. The holy elements were then passed, and I felt that in the hearts of many a worshiper there was a quiet tugging of the heartstrings, a firm resolve to be more worthy of the great sacrifice, and many a renewal of consecration.

When the communion services were over, I found myself inordinately elated to find that Sam was staying to supper at the *Daadihaus*. At least, he hadn't asked to take Eliza Hoffman home—for which I am thankful.

Ya, well, I can't write more now, even though I'd have lots more to write. There's work to do, and next thing, Auntie will be after me with her scathing tongue.

Moonstruck

Annie Petersheim sat at the sewing machine, working at making a new organdy *Kapp* for herself, but her thoughts were on Beccy Eby's journal. Would the stubborn Sam Bricker yet soften to Eliza Hoffman's charms and dowry? Or was he holding out for Beccy?

At last she had the *Kapp* finished, just as Steven was coming in the door. She quickly closed the treadle sewing machine, put some milk on the stove to make hot chocolate, and set out a plateful of chocolate chip cookies, alongside the bowl of shiny red apples.

There should be time for some reading tonight, she thought happily. *Steven has desk work to do—bills to pay and several mail orders to prepare.* Half an hour later she was settling on the settee with her book.

Beccy's next journal entry was the very next day after her last one.

✍

While I wait for the *Schnitzboi* (sliced-apple pie) to finish baking in the cookstove, I'll write more about Sunday. After supper at the *Daadihaus*, Sam sat with Uncle Christian on the back stoop, and they talked until it began to grow dark. Apparently Auntie's suspicions became aroused as to what they were talking about. She bustled outside, determined to investigate. She would have none of this *dumm* Canada talk.

"Why, Sam Bricker," she exclaimed, feigning great surprise, "are you here yet? What will your folks think?"

"It's not dark," Sam replied, "and it's full moon tonight."

"But it's late, almost nine o'clock already," she persisted.

Sam laughed. "So, are you sending me home?"

"Ach, no, not that exactly. You can sit as long as you otherwise can, but Christian must go to bed." She caught Uncle by the elbow and gently but firmly urged him to rise. "Say, what were you two whispering about?" she suddenly asked.

Sam risked no reply, but Uncle bravely admitted, "I was *yuscht* saying, I'm glad Sam's got it in his head to go to Canada."

"So!" Auntie said furiously. "Sam Bricker, you're crazy! What about Eliza Hoffman?"

"She means nothing to me," said Sam.

(With bated breath, I could hear everything through the open kitchen window.)

"But Sam," she persisted, "you could take it easy the rest of your life. And Eliza's a nice girl, I'm sure."

But Sam did not think so. "I don't want a woman with such a *schtruwwlich* (uncombed) head as Eliza."

"She'll comb it if you'll have her, Sam," said Auntie. "She'll do anything for you."

"Will she hike up her petticoats, too, that all the time are peeking out from under her skirts?" Sam said. "No, I don't want her and her *Daadi's* farm."

But Auntie pressed on. "If you don't feel for Eliza, maybe you could find someone else who comes along with a farm."

"Don't want them" was Sam's emphatic reply.

"He's chosen one already," Uncle said hastily, half afraid that Sam would yet succumb to Auntie's grilling.

"And does she have money?" Auntie made bold to inquire.

"Not much," said Sam. "It's Beccy, if she'll have me."

Auntie's face was as black as a thundercloud. Uncle suddenly felt himself gripped by the shoulder and jerked off his chair. "Off to bed with you and your crazy nonsense," she said in an angry voice. "And you, Sam, I never yet sent anyone home, so you can sit here, as I told you before, as long as you otherwise can. But Beccy's not coming out. The *Vollicht* (full moon) has made you *mondgrank* (loony). Good night."

But still Sam sat and waited. He had gained my uncle and guardian's consent, and he felt certain that Uncle would somehow send me out to him, to ask me if I was willing. And then he would have the sole right to sit up with me on Sunday evenings and to take me for drives on Sunday afternoons.

As softly as I could, I opened the front door, tiptoed outside, and sat on the little bench under the apple tree, not visible from Auntie's bedroom window. I waited for Sam. The moon was large and round and red, and it seemed to smile down on the garden. Before long Sam came around the corner of the house and joined me there on the bench, squeezing his large manly form onto the little seat beside me.

We began to talk in low tones. Sam was not practiced in the art of proposing, but somehow or other he worked up the courage to tell me that he loved me and wanted to marry me.

I could not answer right away; my tongue stuck to the roof of my mouth, and a lump formed in my throat. Sam went on to tell of his prospects: "I have no farm and little money. But I have a great idea. In the spring, I want to go to Canada, where others of our people have gone ahead. I will build us a humble home—yours and mine, I hope.

"There would be dangers, loneliness, and labor, with some hardship from being at the outer edge of settled land. At first we would have only silent trees and howling wolves for neighbors, and field and river to supply resources for living."

Finally Sam asked, "Would you be willing to go with me, Beccy? Do you care enough to make the sacrifice?"

I told him, meaning it with all my heart, "I am willing to go anywhere in all the world with you. With you and Menno, I will be happy."

Long into the night we sat and whispered, while the great moon beamed down on us and lit up our happy faces. We surely were moonstruck lovers. But still we had a sense of reality, reckoning with lifelong commitment to each other and the challenge of the Canadian wilderness. Not till the moon began to fade did Sam so much as think of untying Menno and going home.

"Since Auntie gave me permission to 'stay as long as I otherwise can,' I am justified in dallying with you. It is our little joke."

On Monday morning when Auntie found out that we had been "sittin' up" and were already promised to each other, she was white with rage. "You think till spring you're going to Canada, do you?" she said through clenched teeth. "Well, you're not." Again she muttered about "*dumm* Eby notions," but I think she knew then already that she was defeated. The Lord willing, I'm going to Canada with Sam and Menno.

6

Farewells

Beccy Eby must have been quite enthused over Sam Bricker and the proposed journey to Canada. Her journal was bursting with the excitement of it all. Her next entry was the Monday after her second sittin' up with Sam.

Sam's sister-in-law, Annie Bricker, John's wife, came to me to shake hands yesterday after church and to offer congratulations. She said, "I knew something was brewing week before last. Sam sat on the doorstep, alone with his thoughts every evening, whittling away until I had almost enough shavings for kindling to last a year. If he talked at all, it was only to his horse, Menno, who seemed to nod his head from time to time, looking very wise.

"But then last Monday, when Sam came in from the harvest field, he was singing heartily, quite the rapturous lover, and so we knew that he had been sittin' up. When he came to get a drink of water at the pump, just outside the kitchen door, I said, 'You must be feelin' good, Sam, and 'tain't for the good sleep you had, either. John and I heard you come home awful late. By the time you had Menno in the stable, the roosters were crowing already.'

"Sam just laughed good-naturedly and said, 'What would you think, Annie, if I told you I was sittin' up? And that next Sunday can't come around fast enough to suit me?'"

According to Annie, Sam is such an impetuous young man that one can't help but be amused at the ardor of his newfound love. "I always said that when the great passion struck him, it would strike him hard. He told me, 'Beccy's going with me all the way to Canada. It don't give many women like my Beccy!'"

John and Annie happily accepted Sam's choice, but things here at home didn't fare so well, what with Auntie's disapproval. It's not that she is against Sam so much as that she is against the going to Canada. For awhile there, it seemed as though I would be the innocent cause of a family feud. Uncle did all he could to aid and abet us, and Auntie worked just as fervently against us leaving.

Sam was the one who poured oil on the troubled waters and brought peace once more to the household. "I am willing first to go to Canada alone, if need be," he said. "I can buy land, build our cabin and barn, and return in two years for Beccy."

Auntie pondered this proposal and recognized advantages in it that Sam and I couldn't see. "Two years is a long time. Many things can happen—things that might make you change your mind and be satisfied to settle down on a well-cultivated farm such as old Jonas Hoffman would be willing to give you. Everything might come out all right yet in the end."

So she gave her grudging consent. But still she goes around

most of the time wearing a long mouth and a sullen look of disapproval.

I've heard that the idea of migration to Canada is spreading like leaven through the whole community. From those who have already gone, there are glowing reports of marvelous fertility of soil and clear assurances of religious liberty, even better than in Pennsylvania. Here in the war for independence, Mennonites were harassed for staying out of the militia and trying to love the enemy, as Jesus taught.

Last night Sam said, "I wouldn't be surprised to hear that John and Annie might want to go, too, and that Josiah and Susie Schneider are talking about it, too."

Yet there are plenty of others who are voicing their sentiments that Sam is a fool to be reined in, and that I am to be pitied. Ya, well, Sam has enough unbounded enthusiasm for us both. If it's as catching to John and Annie as it is to me, come spring, they'll be headed for Canada, too. I know that I don't have much of an *Aussteuer* (trousseau), but I'll be working at making quilts and a *Deckbett* (coverlet) for our bed, woven in artistic designs.

There's a ferment of excitement here at the Hammer Creek House that is not quenched even by Auntie's dire predictions and maledictions. Uncle Christian is in his element, for it seems to him that at least part of his dream is coming true, now that Sam and I are making plans to go to Canada together. I believe it was what he always wanted for us. People are saying that 'twas Uncle who put Sam up to it, and I know it's partly true. I remember a conversation I overheard between them a while ago. Uncle was urging der glee Bench to go to Canada someday, and then he turned to Sam and said, "Why don't you go, too?"

Sam looked embarrassed and replied, "Me? Ach, I'm not worth much."

"Not worth much!" ejaculated Benj, his eyes alight with admiration for his hero. "Why, you're great!"

But Sam shook his head and said, "I'm not great like you Ebys. Peter can preach, and you and Hannes learn good, but me, I can't be anything but a cucumber of the ground. It's the temper."

"You mean you think that you cumber the ground," laughed

Benj. "But you're no clutter. You're a good farmer."

Sam still looked rather crestfallen until Uncle patted him encouragingly on the shoulder and said, "Anyhow, it doesn't matter whether you are a cucumber or whatever kind of vegetable. Nobody can say what it is worth till it is ripe. And it's a long time till you'll be hauled in, Sam. It's a long time yet till your harvest."

I know Uncle is awfully fond of Sam, even if he does have a temper and is impulsive and impetuous. There is just something about him that is so lovable. Time to go before I write something I don't want anyone else to see.

Spring 1801—Preparations for the trip are beginning in earnest. John and Annie have made up their minds to go, too. "There's the boys to think of," Annie said. "There's little Johnny, a promising lad of eight, and Noah and Moses are younger yet. We can't afford to buy farms for them here. There are no good prospects on this worn-out Bricker farm, nothing to look forward to and hope about. And in Canada, it's mostly all hopes and prospects, 'a land of opportunity,' as John said."

"Think of what fun it will be to dig a farm out of *Buschland* (woodland)," said Sam.

"It will be more than fun," John said. "There will be plenty of hard work. But I doubt that there was a Bricker born yet that was afraid of hard work."

Sam bought a new Conestoga wagon, and John painted his old one so that it looked like new. I helped Annie wrap her china carefully with her household linen. We packed everything in wooden boxes, wondering if the two wagons would hold all they wanted to take along.

The last Wednesday in April is the day chosen as best suited for their departure. The whole community is offering many prayers on the Brickers' behalf, and indeed, their exodus is the chief topic of every conversation, the most remarkable event of the season.

Sometimes I find myself longing to be able to go along with Sam now instead of waiting till he comes back for me. But when I hear of the dangers on the trail, I shrink back in fear. They say there are the all-but-insurmountable Alleghenies to cross, and the Niagara to cross without getting caught in its thundering waterfall.

Also, someone has told us that there's a great boggy swamp that could mire them down if they're not careful. And at any moment, Indians might show up, so they must be alert and friendly. Huge tracts of land have supposedly been purchased from the Indians, but they might still be hunting in the *Busch*. We are pinning our trust on Providence and believe that God will guide the settlers on their journey, and that they will go safely through it all.

✍

April 1801—The great day has dawned at last, and the whole Hammer Creek community has gathered to see the Brickers off. From miles around, the young men have left the farms and their plowing, coming to Brickerville on horseback to see the procession start off.

Auntie was decidedly out of sorts. She kept reminding Uncle that this was what had come of his *dumm* notions, and that if anything happened to the Brickers, he could take the blame. I endured Auntie's mutterings as long as I could, then beat a hasty retreat out the back door. There, under the apple tree, stood the little bench where Sam and I did our settin' up, where we had so often sat together and told each other of our love.

I dropped onto the bench and gave myself up to a flood of memories that rushed in upon my mind. Now I sat alone. I'd have to sit alone and tell my love to the silent stars for the next two years—perhaps forever. My heart was breaking as I heard the Brickers' procession coming, the horses' hooves crunching on the gravel road and the iron-rimmed wagon wheels grinding along.

It was an impressive sight. Each Conestoga wagon, drawn by two pair of heavy draft horses, was covered with a white linen bonnet-shaped top to protect it from sun and rain. The undercarriages and gearings were brilliant red, and the wagon boxes sky blue. Yet there was something so whimsical and substantial about them that they seemed to suit the quaint, puritanical, and thrifty Pennsylvania Dutch folks.

The first wagon was John's. Annie sat on the high seat, hopeful but sad at leaving her relatives and friends. The youngsters were blissfully happy, ready for adventure. Little Johnny sat on the seat beside his father, cracking the whip. When he cried "Whoa!" the horses stopped short, all four of them, right in front of our Hammer Creek House. The cow, trudging behind the Conestoga at rope's end and frisking her tail, had not yet learned the command. The result was a collision, bruising the sleek Jersey's nose.

"Back you," Sam cried. He was following in the second wagon, and that cow was an important part of the procession. She would provide milk and butter for the journey. They would put the cream in a leather bag hung from the back of the wagon, and the motions of the wagon would do the churning and produce butter.

Sam's cargo was mostly tools and livestock, cackling chickens, pigs, and a few frightened sheep. Sam himself sat on a barrel of potatoes and used as his footrest a peck of apple seeds. By careful grafting and budding, he hoped to grow from them an orchard in Canada superior to the best in Pennsylvania.

John and Annie did not alight when the horses stopped. They just leaned out over the wagon box and held out their hands in farewell. I believe the parting was harder than then expected. Tears blinded their eyes, and they could scarcely speak. "Good-bye, Uncle Christian," John succeeded in saying.

"Make it good," said Uncle, deeply moved. "You won't see me again. It won't go long now till I am over there." He motioned to the graveyard over the way.

"And we won't be back," sobbed Annie. The consciousness that she might never again see her friends this side of the river of death dawned upon her as never before, in this last hour of farewell.

"But we'll meet over yonder," Uncle reminded her. The bright hope for that happy day of reunion lit up his face and made it shine as the angels must shine. "It gives another world at the end of this one, thank God," he said.

"We'll look for Beccy to come over pretty soon," said John, seeking to offer his disconsolate wife some comfort more immediate and satisfying in this vale of tears. "Till two years only, isn't it, Sam?" he asked his brother.

Sam had jumped from the wagon to make his farewells. He shook hands with everybody, leaving me till last. "Will you be ready when I come back?" he whispered, holding my hand longer and tighter than the others.

"Ach, Sam, if I was sure that you will come back—"

"Just two years, Beccy," he assured me. "That won't go long."

"A week is long if you don't come," I sighed, remembering how interminable it always seemed from Sunday to Sunday, from one sittin' up to another.

"But every day I'll think about you, and wonder, does everything go good with you?" he said. "And nights when the moon is shining—there's something about the moon that always makes me think about you, Beccy."

"Me too," I said. Looking into his eyes for one more ecstatic moment, I was able to smile.

"We'll have it for a sign between us," he whispered. "The same moon shines in Canada as here. And if it's a full moon, we'll sit up and think of each other. Will you do that, Beccy?"

Such a foolish question. "Of course I will," I replied.

He took me to the back of his wagon and showed me how securely he had tied Menno's halter. I stroked the horse's long white mane and patted his sleek neck. We had a few happy moments to feast our eyes on each other. Our first meeting had been with Menno, out in the barn when Sam had come upon me caressing his horse, his *Schimmel* and mine, and now we had to part in the same way.

Sam was gone before I realized it, and the heavy wheels of the Conestogas were revolving. *Hundli* (little dog, so named), the collie, was running behind, yelping with protest. I turned away, glad that I had been brave in Sam's presence. Not a tear did I shed, nor did a sigh escape me; that would have made it so much harder for Sam. I wanted to steal away alone and cry a great flood of tears, like water when a dam is broken.

No one could ever know how unhappy and anxious I really was, and how empty life had suddenly become. But my tears did not bide their time. My body shook with emotion and sorrow at the parting—fear for his safety and disappointment that I could not go with him. Uncle Christian came and put his arm around me as I sobbed into the elbow of my sleeve.

"Better so," he said consolingly. "Better for both."

I buried my face in his shoulder for awhile till my sobs subsided.

"Better stay here awhile, Beccy," Uncle said, grasping what I was going through. "We don't want her—I mean, you'd best be where there are not so many gapin' at you."

I knew what he meant and was glad enough to sit by the roadside with him, listening to his words of comfort and sympathy. All too soon we'd have to return to the cheerless atmosphere of Auntie's repetitious "I told you so." How little do we know what is in store for us when the great flood of waters comes in and carries us on its bosom out to the deep and boundless sea of life!

○

7

Adventures on the Way

By now Annie Petersheim was so engrossed in the
story that she thought about it all day as she
worked in the house and garden. She tingled with
Beccy's sorrow in parting with Sam as he went on ahead
to Canada. At this point the book shifted from journal
style and was carried by direct narration, with the
storyteller sharing things from various viewpoints.

Whenever Annie could find some free time in the
evenings, she was wrapped up in her book. At mealtimes
and during chores in the barn, she would be telling Steven

snatches of the story. "I can't imagine how Beccy could live apart from Sam for two whole years."

Steven would ask, "Do you want to move to Canada, too? Shall I go over there and look for a farm? I hear that there are horse-and-buggy people like us who are farming and running small shops in rural Ontario."

"No, no," Annie replied. "There is quite enough adventure and wilderness right around here. But I am eager to find out what happens next, and how long it takes for Beccy and Sam to get together again."

So she read on.

✒

The journey upon which the Brickers had set out was full of dangers at every turn and extremely tiresome. When they reached the Susquehanna River, they found that it was even mightier than they had anticipated, a mile wide, and still running high with snowmelt from the mountains. It seemed like an eternity of space lay between them and the farther shore.

A ferry took them across as Annie clasped her baby firmly to her bosom, sure that they were all going to be drowned and end up in a watery grave. Little Johnny's exclamations of wonder and excitement matched Sam's own feeling of high adventure. Both were prepared to enjoy the journey to the full.

Next there were the Alleghenies to cross, and how Annie dreaded that! For a whole week they could see Blue Mountain ahead of them, and at night they saw mountains in their dreams. Utterly insurmountable, they seemed. The nearer the travelers approached them, the more formidable they appeared. At last they reached the foothills and halted for a night of rest before letting the horses start up the perilously steep grade to the summit.

The children were put to bed at sunset, and their elders followed soon afterward. They all were tired and cross and downhearted. Crossing the Alleghenies was a prospect that did not inspire even Sam with abundant hope. It was a monumental challenge.

Little Johnny always slept with Sam and the animals, and

for safety, the two Conestogas were drawn up side by side. The horses had been unhitched, fed, and watered. Sam and John tied them by their halters to nearby trees and blanketed them for a chilly night.

All was quiet, and sleep had come to all but Sam. After a while, he heard a strange sound. He sat up on his bed of boards, cocked his ear, and listened. Again he heard it. What a peculiar sound! Or was it only Annie snoring in a minor key? Quietly, Sam lifted a corner of the linen wagon cover and peeked out. Directly under John's Conestoga, he saw a large dark animal gnawing and crunching the bones that remained from supper. A bear, no less, and not a cub, either!

Sam's heart was in his throat. It would have been bad enough to encounter the brute by day, but to find him snacking under a wagon of sleeping people in the dead of night was another matter. He decided at once that nothing could be gained by sounding an alarm or awakening anybody. He must be especially careful that little Johnny should not be disturbed lest he scream with terror. But how was he to get the intruder to leave?

A bright idea suddenly flashed through Sam's mind. Climbing carefully over the sleeping boy at his side, he reached a box, opened it, and took out one of Annie's hams. He would present this as a peace offering to the bear. Leaning over the edge of the wagon box, Sam tossed the delectable leg of savory meat some distance from the wagon. He saw the monster turn toward the feast spread for him. With gruff, guttural gurglings of relish, the beast devoured it. Then, to Sam's infinite relief, the bear ambled slowly away.

"Is anything wrong?" whispered John, poking his head out of his Conestoga.

"Ach, nothing," replied Sam, as indifferent as he could manage.

"That's what I told Annie, but she is sure it was a bear."

Sam forced a laugh. "Tell her it's nothing to worry about."

John turned to give his wife this comforting message, and soon all was quiet again. But Sam stayed awake and spent the rest of the night on guard against another unwelcome intruder.

The ascent of the Blue Mountain the following day was an

event not soon to be forgotten. It took more than nine hours to travel up the first three miles of the incline. At that rate, the men reckoned, they would never get reach the top. They tried hitching eight horses to one wagon, yet that way they could advance only a short piece before the horses were breathing hard and needed rest to gather strength for another long, steady pull. Later they had to take the teams back for the other wagon.

John was utterly discouraged and ready to turn back to Brickerville. Annie wished devoutly that they had never come. Even Sam's spirits had fallen. Suddenly John gave a triumphant cheer. He had discovered a trail that promised a shortcut through the rocks to the other side. With hope revived, they entered it and followed its curves around masses of solid rock. So narrow was the way and so perpendicular the cliffs, that often to avoid a drop-off, the wagon grazed the rocks on one side, then later on the other. At no point was it possible to see more than a few yards ahead.

Without warning, they suddenly found themselves face-to-face with a stranger coming up from the next valley. There was no room for the rigs to pass each other. This rough, bold fellow announced with a mouthful of profanity that he had the right-of-way. "Back up there, you fool. What do you mean by blocking the road with your Noah's ark?" he bellowed rudely.

"We're loaded," said John, knowing that he had the right-of-way because empty wagons could be moved out of the way easier.

"What do you think you are doing? Moving?"

John nodded. "To Canada."

The rascal laughed loudly with derision. "Canada! You'll never get there. You would do better to turn around now than to wait till later. The bears and wolves will eat you. They like the kids best." He wagged his brushy head in the direction of little Johnny, who was standing with his hands in his pockets. John put his arm protectingly around the boy's shoulder and drew him close.

Sam grunted and said, "Now you know, friend, that since our wagons are loaded, we have the right-of-way. We'll help you take your wagon apart, carry it past, and put it together for you behind us."

"No, no. I can't trust you to help me get going again. You would just take off and leave me stranded with those heavy wagon parts strewn around."

The stranger kept trying to persuade them to turn back. "I know a family that tried to go over this mountain. A pack of wolves fell upon them in the middle of the night and ate up two of the children, plus all the provisions. The parents escaped with their lives but later died of starvation."

"What do you say, Sam? Shall we go back?" asked John, horror-struck at this tale of woe. But with a gesture of impatience, Sam brushed John and his suggestion aside. At his urging, they proceeded to unload the Bricker wagons, dismantle them, and carry them around the stranger's empty wagon. The impudent fellow did not offer to help them assemble and load their wagons.

It was nightfall when the Brickers at last reached the summit of the mountain. Too tired in body to exult in this great accomplishment, they hastened to set up their beds, but the adults were too exhausted to sleep much. All night long, strange noises fell upon their ears. The woods seemed filled with wild animals whose weird cries echoed and reechoed from every side. Even the children were restless and glad to see the morning.

The descent of the mountain was scarcely less arduous and decidedly more perilous than the ascent had been. The weight of the wagons now gave them momentum. Again and again, there was danger that the whole caravan might go tumbling over some precipice to certain death.

It was all the men could do to hold the horses back and pull on the brakes—a lever that pressed blocks of wood hard against the iron rims of the back wheels. Sometimes a slope was so steep that they put a pole through the spokes of the back wheels to lock them and let them drag to slow the wagon, or used a chain to drag a log behind. One place was so bad that they looped a long rope from the rear of a wagon, around a tree, and hitched to Menno, who helped to ease the precious cargo downward.

Next there were dense forests with only a blazed trail and Sam's compass to point the way northwest. The Tonawanda River was another perilous obstacle; its banks were steep and muddy. So, on both sides of the stream, the men felled trees and brush, casting them into the mud and water to make a temporary corduroy incline for the heavy teams and wagons.

Day by day, the road-weary travelers neared the Niagara River. Of all the dangers of the whole journey, there was none that loomed up before their terrified imagination like that mighty river with its swift currents and its great Falls. So many stories of its treachery had reached their ears that they spoke of it in a brooding way as the river of death.

Nevertheless, like death, the Niagara lost much of its terror upon their approach. They came upon it suddenly near its beginning, where the waters of Lake Erie push into the river and flow without noise and tumult, blue as the skies above. There was no sign of the waterfall there. On the other shore they saw Canada, the land of their dreams. Their drooping spirits were revived, and they pressed eagerly forward.

"*Guck mol* (look once), Johnny," cried Sam, with ecstatic joy. "There's Canada!" He lifted the little boy to his shoulder and pointed across the river.

The scenery was majestic as they trekked northward along the Niagara, within sight of its massive rocks and rumbling and tumbling water. Never had they seen such wild beauty before. The climax came when they reached the great waterfalls, with its thundering roar and huge column of mist rising out of the gorge. Speechless, they stood and gazed at the great spectacle, too wonderful for words.

Little Johnny stood quietly beside the men at the spot, which commanded an excellent view of the Canadian Falls. He looked at the great horseshoe shape of the Falls, which his father pointed out to him, and his young head, too, was filled with silent wonder and awe.

The Brickers camped that night within sight and hearing of the waterfall. They could think and talk of nothing else but that miracle of nature stirring the deepest emotions of their souls. It was a beautiful, wonderful, and majestic part of God's good creation.

The next day they pressed on northward along the deep gorge, cut by the river, and eventually came to an Indian village where a group of red men were running the rapids in their

canoes. Beyond that, they neared Lake Ontario and came to quieter water and a convenient landing from which to launch their improvised boats—their wagon boxes, whose seams they had caulked with moss and pitch.

Sam was the first to head across with his horses. They snorted with excitement, and so did Menno, trailing behind. "He'll get himself drowned," shrieked Annie, hiding her face from the horrible catastrophe in the making.

A strong northeast wind gave the adventurer a boost, and his horses played their important parts well, swimming and towing the "boat" across. There were a few anxious moments, when his heart seemed to stand still, what with the rocking "boat," the thrashing horses, and the current. But at last the goal was reached. With a whoop of victory, Sam leaped to the ground and secured one end of a long rope to a sturdy maple tree, ready to help his brother in case of trouble.

Then John felt courage to venture across. It was not long before he found himself out in midstream, battling with wind and wave, and urging his horses onward. The cow bawled her wonder as she swam, too. John landed in safety, in spite of his wife's forebodings.

So there they were at last, a little group of weary immigrants in a foreign land, dumped with their livestock, furniture, and all their worldly possessions on the wild shores of Upper Canada. The trees waved indifferently in the breeze, and the waters murmured monotonously by.

◐

8

The Promised Land

As Annie Petersheim pondered this historic trek of
Lancaster County people to Upper Canada two
centuries earlier, she began to realize that her own
move with Steven to Tennessee was tame by comparison.
They could travel by van to reach their destination and
later to visit the *Freindschaft* back home.

She kept Steven posted on the progress of the story
and soon found another evening to escape to Canada.

It was Saturday night when the weary travelers landed on Canadian soil. Breathing a prayer of thanksgiving, they prepared their beds, stretched their cramped limbs, and watched the new spring foliage of the trees swaying in the breeze. They listened to the murmuring music of the water until eyes and ears were closed in the sweet sweep of sleep and dreams.

Sunday morning, they were up with the sun. They, of course, never traveled on Sunday. It was their day of rest, meditation, and worship. But still, the animals needed to be fed. Sam and John killed several snakes that seemed to infest the region, discovered a spring of fresh and sparkling water to make their oatmeal porridge, and returned to see what Annie was going to give them for breakfast.

"It's the Promised Land," cried Sam, laughing good-naturedly and swinging the water pail. "Look once—there's the Jordan River." He pointed to the Niagara. "Back there's the wilderness. We were forty years in it, not?"

It certainly seemed so, thought Annie.

"More like forty days it was," John said. "Forty days exactly, for I counted them."

Sam was in high spirits. "Come, Johnny, fetch the dishes, and you and I will set the table. Got some *Melassichriwwelboi* (shoofly pie), Annie?"

"*Melassichriwwelboi!*" said Annie. "It'll go a long time till we have that again."

When Sam was drinking the last sip of coffee from his saucer, the importance of this day hit his mind. It was their first morning in Canada. He proposed that they celebrate it in a special way. Sam persuaded Annie to put on her Sunday muslin *Kapp* and told little Johnny to set the folding benches in a row and get out the Bible and hymnbook. He coaxed John into reading the account of the Israelites crossing the Jordan River into the Promised Land. Then they all knelt together and recited the Lord's Prayer.

And how they sang! Sam started the tune as well as he could, while John and Annie and even the children joined in. Soon the woods reverberated with the long-metered hymns of their faith. The birds gathered from all directions as though to help praise their Maker, while the squirrels frisked about from tree to tree in alarm at the invasion.

All day as they rested in their camp, Sam's thoughts kept wandering back to Hammer Creek. Many miles separated him from his Beccy, the girl of his dreams, but he was with her in thought. In his daydreams, he sat beside her on the narrow bench beneath the apple tree. He held her hand, he whispered in her ear, he listened to her sweet confessions of love. Was she ready to go back with him to Canada? Ah, what a wonderful girl was Beccy. He was telling her about a certain little log house that he would build for her. . . .

That evening and part of the night he spent with Menno, the *Schimmel*, and Beccy was with them in spirit, for the moon was full. Only once since they parted had it reached its fullness, and on that night a storm had hidden it from view. But tonight there was scarcely a cloud in the sky. In all of its glory, the great orb of light looked down at Sam and smiled. And Sam looked into its fat, benign face and stayed "as long as he otherwise could."

At daybreak on Monday, they resumed their journey. On Tuesday, little Johnny suddenly emitted a joyful cry: "Look! Smoke!"

Sure enough, there it was—a little blue curl rising from the trees. At last they were nearing "the Twenty," as the new Mennonite settlement was called. It was near Lake Ontario and on the Twenty Mile Creek, so named because of its distance from the Niagara River. They stopped their wagons, and no sooner had the din of wagon wheels died away than there fell upon their ears the welcome sound of a well-swung axe. Chop! Chop!

"Are we here?" asked Annie, a bundle of nerves and excitement.

If John replied at all, it was lost in the volume of noise Sam was making through a funnel he had formed with his hands. "Yoo-hoo! Yoo-hoo!" rang the echo.

The chopping suddenly ceased, and snapping twigs told them that someone was making his way toward them. The next minute there stood before them a tall, well-built, muscular man who bore all the marks of a Mennonite, including a broad-rimmed hat and a shaggy beard, with an axe in hand.

"We're here!" cried Annie. "We're here at last." She heaved a great sigh. Introductions were made, and the woodsman's face beamed with delight. His name was Levi Moyer, originally from Berks County, Pennsylvania.

There was no more wood chopping for him that day. He took them to his humble log home and to his wife, Rachel. It was a pioneer cabin in the heart of the virgin forest, but a happy home for all that. Rachel stood at her doorway to welcome the strangers, shading her eyes with one hand, and supporting her baby on her hip with the other—a bit of Pennsylvania in Canada.

Rachel Moyer gave Annie a hearty welcome. Not every day did she see a woman with a bonnet, though occasionally she saw a squaw. When they had shaken hands, she took Annie to the front room, where she might lay her bonnet and shawl. "It's a cold day for this time of year," she remarked, opening the conversation. "We're getting a breeze from off the lake."

Annie looked up and began to blubber.

"Ach, don't go and cry," said Rachel, patting her on the back. But the counsel was too late. Annie had lost control of herself. She cast herself with abandon on Rachel's breast and sobbed as if her heart would break.

Rachel straightway forgot her own restraint. She threw her arms impulsively around the weeping Annie and mingled her tears with those of her new friend. "I know," she kept repeating. "I know it all."

"I'm so tired," wailed Annie.

"Yes, I know. I don't forget yet what it was like when we came over. I know exactly how you feel. I'll make you a cup of tea. You can *yuscht* sit and eat and rest." She put Annie's baby into the cradle with her own baby and helped the other children take off their wraps.

By morning Annie could not hold her head. The strain of traveling through so many adverse circumstances had overtaxed her physical strength. So Rachel tucked her into her own bed and bestowed upon her sick guest what attention her multiplied duties allowed her, and experimented with all the home remedies she knew.

Sam and John decided to press on further while Annie recuperated. Farther inland, Levi Moyer told them, there was a marvelously fertile region drained by a great river—the Beasley Tract, it was called. Sam, particularly, was intensely interested in settling in this fertile valley. So they set out on horseback.

It was a fortnight before the brothers returned, but they came in high spirits. They had made a bargain, a really good bargain, to judge by their faces. Sam was bubbling over with enthusiasm. He kept patting his bulging waistcoat pocket, secured by a procession of pins, where he carried his precious deed.

They all crowded around the Moyer kitchen table as John and Sam unfolded the papers. The words were long and technical, but the meaning was clear. It was not in vain that John and Sam had skimped and saved on the old farm in Pennsylvania. With the earnings of those lean years, they had each bought three hundred acres of good land at the ridiculously low price of one dollar per acre.

"Landed gentry we now are," Sam took the pains to inform them all. What pleased them most of all was the nature of the soil. It was of a rich, black quality, covered over with giant timbers, the likes of which they had never seen before. They were thinking of the wonderful crops they and their sons would one day raise on land of such amazing fertility.

Levi Moyer was greatly impressed by the price. He was sure that the owner, Richard Beasley, had no idea of the value of the land he was selling at such a figure. Perhaps he had never seen it. But Sam told Levi what he had heard from Beasley's own lips. Beasley assured them that he had visited the tract many times, and that he knew it to be the finest land in all of Upper Canada, purchased from the Six Nations Indians.

"There must be something wrong with it," insisted Levi. "He wouldn't give it away like that unless he is a *Moschkopp* (stupid fellow)."

"Beasley ain't that," interposed John. "He can't be. He's a Member of Parliament."

John sat down in a rocking chair and romped with his boys. "Just think, Little Johnny," said the happy man. "There's a school there already, and a teacher who can learn you good." He had more wonderful tales spun from the bright hopes he had for

55

the land that was to be their home. Little Johnny was an eager listener.

"And we've got good news for you too, Annie," said Sam. "You will have near neighbors, more than a few. I visited very home on the tract, and every woman sent you a friendly greeting and a welcome in advance."

When the men asked Annie how soon she would be ready to start, she declared that she would go in the morning. She was rested up and eager to move ahead now. Nevertheless, when the hour of departure came and the horses were hitched once more to the Conestogas, Annie's heart experienced a certain twinge of regret at leaving the Moyers and the Twenty. "I won't see you no more," said Annie. There were tears in her eyes and sobs in her voice.

"Don't go and cry now, Annie," implored Rachel, clasping her arm. "Look! I picked you some geranium slips." She pressed into Annie's hand a little bundle of plants tied with a moist rag. "Keep the rag wet, and plant them when you arrive. Flowers make such good company. I found that out long already."

Annie took the bundle, stiffened her resolve, and hurried to the door. John had called for her, and little Johnny was cracking the whip in anticipation of departure, and even the cow bawled her impatience.

"Make it good," Levi was saying to the men.

Rachel followed Annie to the Conestoga and watched her climb over the wheel into the wagon. Then she lifted in the small children one by one. "Thank you for the visit, Annie."

"If you could only come and visit me back," said Annie.

The heavy wheels began to revolve. With waving hands, they were off, on their way toward the Promised Land—the Beasley Tract.

◯

<u>9</u>

Log Cabins

Steven was becoming quite interested in the story as Annie shared it with him. He especially liked the search for good land. In fact, he was become so caught up with that epic move to Canada that he even asked Annie to read some of it to him in the evenings.

🖅

Traveling westward along the southern shore of Lake Ontario with Conestogas loaded to capacity became more laborious and perilous the farther they advanced. The horses and even the drivers were tired when they emerged from the marsh at the head (west end) of Lake Ontario. They passed within sight of the palatial home of Richard Beasley and came at last to a little village named Coote's Paradise.

Here they found a church, a mill, a blacksmith shop, a tavern, and a store. The Brickers bought their necessary supplies; it would be their closest store. Only twenty-five miles to go yet! But there was the death trap, Beverly Swamp to cross. Annie's heart sank at the thought of it.

Sam, meanwhile, was bent on a different adventure. He had noticed behind one of the small panes of the store window the words POST OFFICE. Those magic words had stirred up his secret hopes. For once in his life, Sam was a bit nervous. But nevertheless he found that to be a delightfully pleasant sensation.

He darted into an obscure corner of the store, behind a barrel of salt, and stealthily drew out of his pocket a sheet of paper. Sam looked about cautiously and assured himself that he was alone and unobserved. He reached for the quill and bottle of ink that stood on the proprietor's desk nearby, and as fast as his unskilled fingers could convey words to paper, he wrote:

Dear Beccy,
I must write a cupple lines so that you know we live yet, & goes everything good so far. Annie was sick by Levi Moyers at the Twenty, but she is good again. I bot 300 akers & John the same. It is on the Grand River. Last night it was our full moon.
    Your Sam

It was the document of a thousand loving thoughts, this first love letter that he had ever written, and it gave him such agreeable palpitations of the heart. But when the haughty postmistress snippily informed him that it would cost a dollar to mail it, Sam slunk out of the store with a heavy heart, deciding that it wasn't worth that much.

Two hours later, the Brickers left Coote's Paradise and were on their way to find their own paradise in the Beasley Tract. They were going by the direct route, northwest through the

Beverly Swamp, all twenty-five miles of it. If Annie was any sort of prophetess, they were about to be buried alive. Worst of it all was that nobody would ever know when or where the final struggle would be.

Poor John had to listen to Annie's fears and complaints day after day, but Sam led on, blissfully immune to the influence of Annie's fears. Only the grunts of the pigs and the cackle of the hens disturbed his peace. On the third day, an interminable rain set in, and soon the swamp was a veritable bog. Then even Sam began to look serious and wonder if their days were numbered.

They were in constant danger of losing their way because the vegetation was so lush that it hid the path in many places, and on every hand there were yawning wet deathtraps half concealed by shrubbery. The men lost their tempers times without number, and Annie kept reminding them, "I told you it would be bad. Why did we ever leave Pennsylvania?" Oh, to be able to go anywhere in the whole wide world—anywhere, as long as they had the assurance that they would never again hear of the Beverly Swamp.

It took them a week to get through the swamp. There is an end to every road, and it comes at last with patience. They reached firmer ground, and the sun shone once more with warmth. Immediately their flagging spirits began to revive. Directly ahead flowed the Grand River on its way southward to Lake Erie. Now the party of new settlers were within a few miles of their destination. The day of realizing their hopes was at hand.

A royal welcome awaited them. The Betzners, the Sherks, the Bechtels, the Gingrichs, the Livergoods, the Shupes, the Rosenbergers, the Reicherts, and the Suraruses opened their homes to them and showed them a thousand kindnesses. Annie met the women who had sent her kindly messages, and little Johnny met his teacher, David Rittenhouse, and some of his future schoolmates. Everyone had a hearty handshake and a cheerful greeting of welcome for the newcomers.

They worshiped with this group of Mennonites and with them sang the praises of the great God, who had made them to lie down in green pastures and beside the still waters. They were in their Promised Land and were part of the first settlement of

Europeans inland in Upper Canada, away from the lakes.

Autumn had come, and winter was fast approaching. The Brickers knew they must lose no time in making preparations for building unless they wanted to live all winter in their Conestogas. So they went to work with a will. Day by day, resounding through the empty forest were the sound of the axe, the crash of falling timbers, and the echoes of cheerful song.

The site that John had chosen was near Sam Betzners, and there they made the first clearing. First they built a stable for the horses, and next the house, with vertical logs for framework around doors and windows, and horizontal logs for the walls. Spliced logs were slanted at the right angle for the roof. Bark, twigs, and mud filled each chink and cranny. When it was finished, a cheery fire blazed in the fireplace, made of large stones from the riverbed, fitted together with fieldstone. On the floor they laid strips of rag carpet and handwoven mats.

These were crude furnishings, to be sure, but the hearts of these pioneers beat high with hope. Not even the rigors of a Canadian winter could dampen the ardor of these dauntless settlers. Even if nature was unfriendly, hope was strong and buoyant.

It was February before anyone but Sam himself had time to think of Sam's house. He had chosen a spot on the east side of the river, three miles further north than anyone had yet ventured to settle. Day after day, Sam and John trudged their way through the snow to this place that Sam called his *Bauerei* (farm). All day long, from dawn till sunset, they felled the timbers that were to find a place in Sam's forest home.

Those were tedious days for Annie. She saw the men at breakfast and supper, then endured ten long, lonely hours between, with only the prattle of the children to break the silence. Many a silent tear she shed: it was hard—nobody knew how hard it was here in the wilderness—but she must be brave.

The winter of 1802–1803 brought terrible anxiety and suffering to the Mennonites on the Beasley Tract. The crops had been poor, hungry wolves howled for vengeance, and the winter was long and bitterly cold. More than one family looked starvation in the face. But they were a community of brothers and sisters, so they shared even to their last crust. Potatoes were so scarce that even the peelings had to be saved for planting in the spring. There was much relief when spring came before any of their number had succumbed to the cruel winter.

There was no end of trouble in building Sam's house, too. Every other day Sam kept changing his mind about the plans. When he had chosen the site, he found that a huge oak of marvelous girth had years before staked out that claim. John laid his axe to the root of the tree, but Sam stopped him. He wanted it cut at the right height so that the stump would support Beccy's tabletop, and the house must be built around it.

Every log had to reach a certain standard, or Sam would reject it. No knotty, misshapen logs should house his Beccy. John had to put up with it all. His brother's notions amused him. "You would have saved yourself a lot of bother, Sam," he said one day, "if you would've fetched her along over. Once you are married, you won't have to ask her where she wants the chimney or how high the table must be. She'd *yuscht* take what you give her and be thankful."

These and similar taunts, Sam bore with considerable good humor, and before the summer came, Beccy's house was ready, awaiting her coming. The spring of 1803 brought more settlers to the Beasley Tract. With each successive week came new Conestogas, and there was a welcome for all.

The older settlers offered timely advice and assistance. The newcomers gratefully received all these overtures of friendship and kept up the practice of helping each other in the community. A new Pennsylvania was emerging in the heart of Upper Canada, a new Pennsylvania with the same people, the same traditions, and the same religious faith as in the old Mennonite settlements of eastern Pennsylvania.

○

10

Duped

Steven and Annie Petersheim were on their way home from a trip to the grocery story in Willowcreek. "C'mon, Rusty." Steven flicked the reins on the horse's back. "We want to get home before the rain arrives. Maybe we should've used the *Dachweggeli* (roofed buggy) instead of the trottin' buggy. We sure are having a lot of cloudy and rainy days these past few weeks."

"More rain, more rest," quoted Annie. "I've gotten my quilt out of the frame now, and so with some free time, maybe I can get the Sam Bricker book finished soon."

"Oh, Sam," Steven chuckled. "Is he about ready to go back to Pennsylvania to fetch his Beccy over to Canada?"

"Not yet, but he has the cabin built for her now. Let me catch you up on the story that I have read thus far. Those poor Mennonite settlers sure fell into dire times and misfortunes."

"How so?" Steven was surprised. "You mean something worse than the near starvation they faced that first hard winter?"

"Yes. They found out that they'd been cheated. The deeds to the land they'd bought were worthless, and their hard-earned money was lost. They weren't at all the owners of the acreage they were farming and had built their houses and barns on.

"Richard Beasley turned out to be a crook. He had pocketed their money and issued deeds that were fakes because he had a mortgage on the tract and still owed money to the Indians for it. No wonder he was willing to sell valuable land at a dollar an acre."

"Whew!" Steven sputtered. "How did they find it out?"

"It was Sam Bricker who made the discovery. Let me tell you the story as we head for home," said Annie.

✍

Sam wanted to see muddy little York (now Toronto), the capital of Upper Canada, sixty miles away as a crow flies. John needed another cow, and Sam offered to buy one for him in York. So on a bright September morning in 1803, he set out on foot.

At York, Sam met a man named Jim Wilson, an honest and straightforward fellow. He knew about Richard Beasley's dishonest dealings with the Mennonites, and as he gazed into Sam's earnest, honest face, he sensed that he had a guileless heart and a conscience void of offense toward God and fellow human beings. Behind his frank and open countenance, Jim thought, there could not lurk any hidden sin or dishonesty. He knew that martyr blood of the centuries flowed in his veins, something more valuable than worldly honor.

So Jim resolved to tell Sam the whole truth before Sam returned to his home. He told Sam not to leave before he came back to talk to him again.

Meanwhile, Sam set out to inquire about buying a cow. He fell in with an obliging wag of a man who said his name was Peter Potter, and that his job was selling ideas to people who didn't have any. Peter said he would show Sam around in York, then take him to an auction barn where he could buy a cow. In return, Sam offered to buy him his dinner.

At the dinner table, Peter, with ulterior motives in mind, ordered a pint of rum for Sam, and he made sure that Sam emptied the mug. He had slyly said it was his treat, but he let Sam pay the bill.

After dinner, they went to the sale, and soon the fun began. There was only one cow there, and it was a bundle of skin and bones. Peter urged him to buy her, saying that it was a bargain. Sam's poor rum-befuddled judgment could not resist, and he bought her for fifteen dollars—a lot of money for that time.

Gradually it dawned on Sam that he had been swindled. Behind his back, Peter had raised the bid, then pocketed the money, and the cow was worthless. Sam's temper was aroused, and it was just as well that Peter had disappeared by then.

After a sleepless night, Sam started to the stable for the scarecrow cow, wondering how he would ever explain things to his brother. At the gate he met Jim Wilson, who told him the story of the Beasley Tract—how Richard Beasley had cheated them. They owned no land at all, and besides that, there was a mortgage for ten thousand pounds on the tract. Beasley himself had simply written the deeds, and they were defective.

Sam couldn't believe it. "You lie," he said, "and if I were you, I'd get my head charmed once."

But Wilson insisted that he was telling the truth, and that Sam could go to the Registry Office and see for himself. At last Sam agreed to check it out, and there he learned that Jim Wilson had told the truth. There were no records of sales of any portion of the Beasley Tract, and it was mortgaged for ten thousand pounds, money owed to the Six Nations Indians.

"But I bought three hundred acres from Beasley, and I have the deed," Sam told Mr. Ridout, the registrar. The registrar shrugged his shoulders and said, "If you have a deed, it isn't worth the paper it's written on." The registrar wondered what would happen, knowing that the Mennonites wouldn't take the offensive.

Sam actually staggered under the blow. And then his temper flared. With clenched fists and lightning darting from his eyes, he rushed from the registrar's office, heading for Beasley's place at the head of the lake, thirty-five miles west of York.

With great disgust, he remembered the skinny cow. He grabbed her halter, half dragging her with herculean strength on his way. The cow held back at first, then changing her tactics, she ran as fast as she could, tugging the distressed and wrathful Sam along. This tug of war between Sam and the cow didn't improve Sam's humor, but it did wear him down and help him to gain control of his temper.

When evening came, Sam found a resting place under some trees by the roadside. He knew that he wouldn't sleep, but he was thinking and planning. "O Lord, help me," he cried aloud. He could say no more because a great lump filled his throat and choked his utterance.

O

Annie paused in her story to ask Steven, "Do you think Sam's impulsive temper really came from having red hair? Do red-headed people have more fiery tempers than others?"

"I don't know, but I don't believe so," Steven replied. "Sam really had something to be mad about, and all of us have tempers if we're provoked far enough. I might've done worse than Sam. What happened next?"

"Well, Sam was exceedingly worried."

✍

Sam had thought he had three hundred acres and a house for his Beccy, and now it was all gone. Would she consent to marry a homeless, penniless man? They might starve together. What's more, in the morning he found the skinny cow dead, her tongue protruding from between her teeth. He kicked her hated carcass, but then realized that the cloud had a silver lining. Perhaps now he could suppress the story of Peter Potter and the auction sale.

So, empty-handed, he journeyed on, and in the afternoon of the third day he reached Beasley's mansion at the head of the lake. Sam knocked on the door.

He saw a curtain flutter at a window, and then he heard a woman's voice: "Another Dutchman, Richard! Be sure he wipes his feet before you let him in. And whatever you do, don't invite him for dinner!"

Beasley came to the door and ushered him in. Sam confronted the man, at first craftily, then none too gently.

"What's your name?" Beasley asked him.

"Sam Bricker, come last year from Lancaster County, Pennsylvania," Sam replied.

"I remember that there were two Brickers here in the spring of last year, one married and one single. The younger one had red hair and looked a lot like you. Your brother or cousin, perhaps?"

"No," Sam replied.

"But surely you know him. You Mennonites are all connected one way or another."

Then Sam, like David confronting Goliath, picked up the first little stone: "I know him better than most people, and he cheats easy."

"You don't say!" exclaimed Beasley, bristling with suspicion. "Now that you mention it, he did look as though he might be crooked. Something of a devil, is he?"

"A devil!" shouted Sam. "Is that what you call him?" With difficulty, he kept his hands off the man.

Beasley hastily replied, "Well, I guess *devil* is the wrong word." With a nervous laugh, he added, "I don't suppose I'll be having any more dealings with him. He's back on the tract in his little shanty, no doubt, happy as a clam."

"A happy home, you think? On your mortgaged land?" Sam gazed steadily at Beasley until he knew satisfaction of seeing the color come and go on the face of the guilty man. The second stone had struck its mark.

"My word! Who are you that you dare to speak so to me?"

"I am the devil!" roared Sam.

"Yes, yes," mocked Beasley. "You roar like one."

"The devil will have his own!" shouted Sam. He sprang from his chair and strode across the room with determination.

Rather weakly, Beasley ordered Sam to leave the house. But Sam stood with his back toward the door and refused to leave. At that moment a frightened feminine voice called, "Richard, dear, come here at once. I want you."

Under the spell of that voice, Beasley darted to the staircase and banged the door after him, evidently fearing that the Mennonite might include himself in the woman's timely invitation. Sam noiselessly let himself out the front door and ran to the back door, which he propped shut, against any hope of Beasley's escape. He closed all the first-floor shutters and secured them from the outside, then resumed his stand before the front door. Barring a jump from an upstairs window, Beasley must sooner or later meet him there.

Fully half an hour Sam waited. At last Beasley came downstairs, wearing an air of offended dignity. Seeing that his dishonesty had been revealed, and surmising that the Mennonites were gullible people, he made Sam an offer. He would give back the three hundred dollars he had paid for his acreage if he would go back to the tract and keep his mouth shut about the dishonesty and the mortgage.

Beasley wrote an order for three hundred dollars and pressed it into Sam's hand. But Sam straightened himself up and without so much as looking at Beasley, tore it into ribbons and said, "I would rather lose all I have—I'd rather die—than do that."

Next Beasley asked, "What if I return the money to all of you? What then?"

"I suppose we'd all have to go back to Pennsylvania," Sam said, "or buy land somewhere else in Canada."

Beasley was shrewd and did not want another man to reap the benefits of his dishonesty. Neither did he want a pack of Mennonites to bespatter his fair name. He thought for a moment and then said, "Raise ten thousand pounds, and I'll pay off the mortgage and give you a clear title to sixty thousand acres. I'll give you two years to come up with the money."

Sam gasped. Ten thousand pounds was a fabulous sum, equal to about fifty thousand dollars.

"Your friends in Pennsylvania have money," Beasley told him. "Go over there and get them to form a land company and buy the tract. When the bargain is closed, I'll give you five hundred acres of your choosing. That's the best I can do."

Sam's eyes fairly danced with excitement as he started back to his people on the Beasley Tract. That was a huge spread of beautiful land, all for less than a dollar an acre. When Sam reached home and told the whole story, however, a terrible consternation fell on the poor, deluded people. The news spread like wildfire to all the homes in the settlement. Would to God they had stayed in Pennsylvania instead of coming to Canada—this land of blasted hopes.

But Sam refused to be dejected. He was determined to go back to Pennsylvania, raise the money, clear the land of the mortgage, and get those five hundred acres Beasley had offered him. He called a meeting at John's house, and there he told them of his idea, to raise the money in Pennsylvania.

At first the men remained in utter despair, thinking it useless even to ask the fellow Mennonites back in Pennsylvania for help. Some even talked of moving back to Pennsylvania that fall yet. But when Joseph Sherk, levelheaded and respected by all, offered to go to Pennsylvania with the impulsive Sam, their opinion changed. They would wait and see. Hope began to revive.

A delegation of settlers went back to Beasley that fall and negotiated carefully. When the Erb brothers finally had the papers all ready for signatures, Beasley would not sign. He declared that he had offered no such bargain to Sam, and that Sam was a confounded liar and firebrand. If Sam thought he was getting the finest tract in all of Upper Canada for a song, he didn't know Richard Beasley.

When Sam heard this report, he was so enraged at Beasley's lies that he started at once toward the head of the lake, to confront him at his mansion. But a terrible snowstorm blew up and blocked the roads. Three times he started off, but each time had to return.

Later the Erb brothers went with Sam and strengthened his cause with Beasley. By this time, Beasley was running out of luck, with creditors hounding his heels. Jim Wilson threatened him with public exposure for his cheating if he persisted in refusing to live up to his bargain: "Mennonites will never buy another acre from you. The name of Richard Beasley, Member of Parliament, will be a black mark on the page when the colony's history is written."

Beasley swore profusely and cursed Sam as a robber, but he finally dipped his quill pen into the ink and signed his name. All this followed days of stiff bargaining, overseen by a trustee for the Indians, who were holding Beasley's mortgage. The Erb brothers agreed to pay the ten thousand pounds by installments within the two-year limit, as Beasley had proposed.

Daniel Erb signed the preliminary purchase agreement on November 28, 1803. He and his fellow settlers had faith that the Mennonite *Freindschaft* (church family) in Pennsylvania would help them accomplish the deal. But if the Mennonites could not produce the money in time, the deal would fall through, and the settlers would lose their land and buildings.

It was decided that Joseph Sherk and Sam Bricker would start off for Pennsylvania the next Monday morning, to appeal for aid. At the first opportunity, Sam hurried to the barn to tell Menno about it. He smiled as he patted the *Schimmel's* white mane and whispered a name they both held dear. They were going to Hammer Creek and to Beccy.

◗

11

Hard Times

Annie continued telling Steven more of the story at the supper table. They were wondering how Sam Bricker and Joseph Sherk would make out when they arrived at Hammer Creek to ask for money. Would Lancaster Mennonites recognize the value of land and forests in far-off Canada?

As soon as the chores were done, Annie got the book to read more. To her surprise, Steven moved his chair close beside her at the kitchen table, and so they read together in the lamplight.

After Sam Bricker and Joseph Sherk left for Pennsylvania, the weather turned nasty. Never before in all their experience in Upper Canada were the days so melancholy as those that visited the settlers on the mortgaged Beasley Tract during the fall and winter of 1803–1804. The clouds hung thick and heavy, and rain fell for days at a time. The wind moaned in the trees, the sun refused to shine, and a terrible gloom fell like a pall over all the land. Snow came early, drifted deeply, and stayed.

The distressed people gathered as usual for worship. With tears in their eyes, they prayed on bended knees for God's mercy. "O Lord, incline the hearts of our friends in Pennsylvania to come to our aid." They prayed for wisdom and favor in behalf of Sam Bricker and Joseph Sherk.

Nor did they forget Richard Beasley, the man who had swindled them. "Oh that you, the great wonder-working God, would dissolve his heart into penitence so that he might cry aloud for forgiveness and find rest for his sin-cursed soul." Weak and impotent they were of themselves, but they were the children of the almighty God. They brought their case to the Lord, and they were willing to leave it in his hands. "Let your will, not ours, be done."

John's wife Annie had never really recovered from the mental and physical strain of the journey to Canada. She longed for the homeland with an irrepressible yearning. Not even the geranium slips from Rachel Moyer could cheer her. Annie had a bad case of *Heemweh* (homesickness), and she was sure that she would never be happy again until she could go back to Hammer Creek.

O

Steven noticed that Annie had finished reading the page long before he did. He got up and chose a shiny red apple from the bowl. "It's no use, Annie, I can't keep up. I guess you'll have to read the story aloud to me."

His eyes twinkled as he smiled at his wife. "So John Annie had the *Heemweh.* Maybe she was a little like another Annie I know—an Annie Petersheim. Weren't you feeling the same way for a while when we first came to Willowcreek Valley?"

"Well, not that bad," Annie said briskly, though she felt herself blushing. "I always liked it here in Tennessee, but leaving the dear ones back home was hard at first." Then she added, "However, I do feel sorry for what Annie Bricker had to endure. I peeked ahead, and it looks like the worst is yet to come. Okay, if you want me to, I'll read aloud for awhile."

✍

Little Johnny Bricker, the apple of his parents' eyes, came down with diphtheria. He tossed and tumbled about in his bed, muttering all sorts of incoherent things in his delirium. He had started out with a sore throat, and his mother wrapped a stocking around his neck, patted his cheek, and told him it would be better in the morning. But he got worse, and there were two large white spots in his throat, which was swollen and inflamed.

It was the dreaded diphtheria. What a blow for John, too. He had entertained such fond hopes for this precious lamb of their fold. If only there was something he could do.

There was! The sulfur! He sent all the children into the bedroom and went in himself, bearing a shovelful of burning coals from the fireplace in one hand, and a tin can in the other. He closed the door and commanded them all to open their mouths as wide as they could and inhale. Then he dropped the yellow powder from the box onto the glowing coals. A blue smoke arose and pervaded the room: it was supposed to kill the diphtheria germs.

Annie always blamed the sulfur as much as the diphtheria for the death of little Johnny. The poor fellow coughed away all his strength. The grief of the parents knew no bounds. In the weeks that followed, a terrible diphtheria epidemic spread through the settlement, and scarcely a home was left unscathed. Was God dead, or why had he forsaken them?

Into this deepest gloom was born the second little Johnny Bricker. He was a puny child, not make to face the rigors of a Canadian winter. In less than a month they had to bury him,

beside the original little Johnny, whom he had never seen.

Annie's heart was all but broken. When the last guest had departed after the funeral, she wrapped herself in her great shawl and wandered off alone to the little graveyard on the hill. Here on the summit she had made for herself a place of retreat last summer already. She had planted Rachel's geraniums out for the summer and fashioned for herself a little seat. Far below, around many a graceful curve, the river had murmured by, but now it was silent, covered with ice.

Here they had scraped back the snow and chopped through the frozen ground to bury the two little Johnnies in this strange mortgage-cursed land. In the spring the flowers would bloom again, though all who loved them would be far away. Perhaps the birds would come and perch on the seat and sing a song over the poor little neglected graves.

Annie stood beside the graves and sobbed. How cold their little bodies must be in the frozen earth. If only she could fold them to the warmth of her bosom. "O God!" she cried, throwing an agonizing glance to the blue skies above, weeping heartbrokenly. Her whole frame shook with pent-up emotions.

Suddenly she felt a Presence. A voice, sweet as an angel's, was calling her name. A great peace overwhelmed her. "Ah, God is still with me."

"Annie!"

She looked up and saw a heaven-sent angel—John, leaning over her. His great arm tightened around her shoulders, and her head dropped on her husband's bosom. "You don't know how hard it is," she sobbed.

John's own heart was breaking with grief. "Annie," he whispered, "I'm afraid I might lose you too. Then what would I do?"

Annie was quiet for a moment before she said, "And I didn't even think about you, John." She dropped her head again on his shoulder and let him draw her close into the shelter of his arms. A strange glow warmed her heart. There, beside the little graves, she had found true happiness—healing for her soul, such as she had never known before in her life.

Before that winter was over, the dwellers on the Beasley Tract again faced the wolves of starvation. When things came to the worst, they went to Coote's Paradise and begged for flour. They would pay when they could.

In April, Joseph Sherk returned alone. One glance at his face, and their last, lingering hope died away. He had visited Franklin and Cumberland Counties, calling upon all the wealthy Mennonites he knew, but with no success. They would not listen to his entreaties. Some had even laughed.

"Even if we had money to throw away, why should we send it to Canada to enrich a man who has already proved himself to be a rogue? There are plenty of good causes in our own young country, at our very doorstep. Better pack up and come back to Pennsylvania," they advised him. "If you do come back, you will find plenty of sympathy and support."

So now the settlers on the Beasley Tract had their fears confirmed. "Where's Sam?" asked John Bricker with a sigh. "Is he sick maybe?"

"Ach, Sam," replied Joseph. "He thinks he knows a man in Lancaster County who might help. Christian Eby of Hammer Creek."

"He might," John allowed, "if his *Fraa* (wife) would let him. But she won't. If Sam went there, he'll take Eliza Hoffman and her *Daadi's* farm, and we won't see him any more."

So the settlers abandoned every hope of help and made preparations to leave the Beasley Tract. Early in May, they were to set out together one morning for the homeland. The Conestogas were brought forth and drawn up before the houses, and the packing began. But this time, there was no happy, buoyant heart in all the company. The spirit of adventure was dead in them: they had failed and were returning beaten and penniless.

On their last day they were to spend on the Beasley Tract, Annie acted quite strange. She scarcely spoke to her husband and children, but walked like a ghost among them. When evening came on, John saw her take the trail that led to the retreat on the hill.

Poor Annie, he thought. *She's so torn between grief and* Heemweh.

Annie stumbled into the little enclosure and fell prostrate between the two little mounds. She poured out her heart in tears and prayers. John was anxious for her. He came and knelt beside her and put his arm protectingly about her.

"Ach, John, I can't let them here," she wailed. "I can't go away and let them here."

John racked his brain for some consoling thought. "We must mark the graves," he said. "Someday, perhaps, we can come back and see them." But in his heart of hearts, he knew that was foolish talk.

Yet the idea took hold of Annie. Yes, they must mark the graves, not with slabs of wood or stone—they are so cold and lifeless—but with something that will live and grow through the years like her memories.

"A sapling is the very thing. Let's plant it together between the graves. In time it will become a mighty oak. The more it stretches its limbs toward the heavens, the deeper it will send its roots into the earth. In time they will encircle the bodies of my boys in place of their mother's arms."

To humor her, John planted the tree. But he was more anxious about Annie than he cared to confess. He was glad they were going back to Pennsylvania, and he hoped that when she got back among her friends, Annie would not have such strange thoughts. She would be her old self again, instead of this bundle of nerves and weird ideas. But who could blame her, thinking of all she had gone through?

O

12

Christian Duty

The next evening when Annie Petersheim started reading to Steven, she noticed that Beccy Eby's journal was now picking up the story. "Well, Steven, this should be exciting. I wonder how Beccy and Sam get along with each other now. Let's see if true love conquers all."

"What I want to know," said Steven, "is whether they can raise the money to pay off the mortgage. You have to have land to support love."

"Ya, well. Always the true farmer, aren't you?"

Hammer Creek House, early spring 1804—Sam and Menno are back at last, and my cup of joy is full and running over! He was here for church services, and we had our first settin' up together last night. Auntie did not invite Sam to stay for supper, but he overlooked the little omission, helped himself to a plate from the cupboard, and squeezed in beside Benj.

In spite of Auntie's glowering face, we were hilariously happy. Sam joked about everything and kept me suffused with radiant blushes. Benj begged him for the story of his adventures. How we all hung on to his words as he described crossing the Alleghenies, the arduous trekking through the wilderness with the Conestogas, and the terror of the wild animals. We listened with rapt wonder as he described the thundering Niagara, the giant growth of timbers, and the marvelous fertility of soil in Canada.

"Now tell me: did Annie get *Heemweh?*" Auntie demanded to know. "If she's got it, it serves her right, and if she doesn't have it, I'm sure she soon will. Has she got it, eh?"

Sam had to confess that Annie was suffering from homesickness. "But she will be better when Beccy arrives."

Auntie cooed with satisfaction. "I told her so, but she wouldn't hear it. You'll get it, too, Beccy," she told me.

Right then, I wanted nothing so much in all the world as a place to hide my burning face. But Sam didn't seem to mind. It seemed that nothing could dash his high spirits.

After everyone else retired for the night and we were finally left alone, he, the happy lover, whispered to me, "You don't want me to go yet, do you, Beccy?"

I smiled, remembering our little joke, and said, "You know that you dare stay as long as you otherwise can." That ungracious permission of Auntie's has brought us so much happiness. We talked awhile in whispers, and then Sam said, "Fetch your shawl once, Beccy. I want to see how the old apple tree looks."

Hand-in-hand we walked out to the garden and stood on the spot where the bench had held us on that memorable night when first we mutually confided our love. Again his strong right arm encircled my shoulders, and again we renewed our plighted troth.

"It's not grand, . . . my *Aussteuer* (trousseau), Sam," I told him. "Now if it was Eliza Hoffman's—"

"Eliza Hoffman," he scoffed. "Who wants her and her *Aussteuer*? Nobody wants her even with all her farms, it seems."

"It's her own fault," I told him. "She won't take anyone else—she wants you."

Sam made a gesture of impatience. "It's a good thing we are going away so soon. By next week, we must go."

"Ach, Sam," I murmured and clung to him, loving him better than all the rest of the world.

We moved around the corner of the house and saw, low on the horizon, a great full-orbed moon. It was actually smiling at us and nodding with approval. "Glad to see you two there again," it seemed to say. "My blessings on you both."

Then Sam told me what the moon had meant to him during the lonely hours of his absence from me. He said, "I never looked at it but that it brought to me sweet memories of a certain lovely girl at Hammer Creek. If it happened to be full, I stayed up half the night, living over again a certain happy experience."

I told him, "We must be a pair of silly Canada geese, for I did the same things."

When he told me that within a week we would be on our way to Canada, my heart seemed to turn over. I knew that I loved him dearly, but was I really ready to go so far away with him to the wilds of Upper Canada?

Sam didn't seem to mind that my *Aussteuer* was scanty, that I'm just a poor little orphaned Mennonite girl, and that I have no costly china cabinets of silver and embroidered linens. All I have in my cedar chest is just a collection of hand-patched quilts, a *Deckbett* (coverlet), and a few rag mats and homespun towels. But I have a wealth of happiness that fills my heart.

What do such things matter when I have a man like Sam? He is a real hero now, chosen to take twenty thousand dollars along to Canada. Let me explain how this happened.

When our people learned of the plight of our brothers and sisters in Canada, Hannes Eby and others urged the bishop and ministers to call a meeting at Hammer Creek House, where

Hannes lived. His father, Christian, came over from the *Daadihaus* and joined the men gathering in the living room. We women were in the huge kitchen, with the doors open so we could hear and see. I watched as the men found places on the benches and chairs. But I really had eyes for only one—Sam, arriving on the *Schimmel,* my Menno.

I made myself comfortable on the woodbox behind the kitchen stove and made sure to be in a line of sight to watch Sam through a door. First we sang awhile, then knelt in prayer. Christian's son Peter Eby, now a bishop, was leading the prayer, telling the Lord that they wanted everything that was done to bring him glory.

After the prayer Sam got up to speak. His eyes were closed at first, and he was breathing heavily, for he is a man of action rather than of words. But soon he forgot himself, so earnest was he for the cause he represented. His plea for help was eloquent, and expressive gestures came to his aid when words failed.

Sam told about the privations and want in Canada, the howling wolves and prowling wildcats, hard winters and forest fires. "But it is all a goodly land, flowing with milk and honey. Right now a mortgage hangs over it like a pall, but that could eventually prove to be a blessing in disguise," Sam predicted.

"We can depend upon the British government to keep its sacred promises to us Mennonites, to grant us freedom of religion. The officials have said that we will be exempt from the military because of our conscience against war. So no one will hassle us for following Jesus, who told us to love our enemies.

"We settlers in Upper Canada have gone ahead like the spies sent to scout out the Promised Land. I challenge you to go up to this land, for we are well able to possess it. Imagine—six hundred thousand acres are in the deal, at less than a dollar an acre. This will make enough farms for our children to the fourth generation and more. The Lord God will be with us as truly as he was with the Israelites of old when they were obedient."

I was fully persuaded by Sam's speech. But poor Sam, by reading the expression on the bishop's face, seemed to sense that he had failed even before any vote was taken. He sat down dejectedly and listened to the trite words of Bishop Peter.

The bishop had not a shred of confidence in Sam's petition.

"What sense does it make to risk more lives on such dangerous treks? Why would more families want to try to hack out a living in such a bleak wilderness, in the great white North? If more farmland is needed, why not go west right here in green Pennsylvania?

"Let them come back to Pennsylvania, a land we know God is blessing. That would make more sense, and we would be within reach to help each other. What we can offer for the settlers on the Beasley Tract is the consolation of our prayers—but no pledges of money."

However, it was not just prayers that Sam had come from Canada to solicit. He was downright discouraged.

Away back on the Beasley Tract, people righteous and true had for weeks been besieging the throne of grace with fervent prayers for his success. But what was the use of praying, anyhow, if God would not grant the earnest entreaties of an innocent, betrayed people? What was God's will in this matter?

Yet Sam, as usual, had been too hasty in his judgments. Even at the eleventh hour, the Lord answered the prayers of his distressed people. The bishop was about to pronounce the benediction when his brother Hannes Eby gave a sign of dissent and walked to the front of the room. He reached for the Bible on the shelf and turned the pages till he found his verse: "Whoever has pity on the poor, lends to the Lord, and the Lord will repay him what he has given" (Proverbs 19:17). "This," he announced, "is a harness peg upon which I wish to hang a few remarks.

"I do not think we have considered Sam's proposition in the right light," Hannes said. "Instead of looking upon it as a speculation to enrich ourselves, which it likely would not do, we should regard it as our Christian duty to assist, if possible, our friends in distress. If it yields us no financial profit, we would at least be doing our duty, an act that the Lord might, in his own good time, bless in a way none of us can imagine now. I would leave the matter to each man's conscience."

A new light shone in Sam's face, and his eyes sparkled with hope when Uncle Christian got up and said, "I want to help our brethren in Canada. I pledge $2,500." Others followed suit with substantial pledges.

"*Dumm!*" muttered Auntie in the kitchen. "What won't that

man all do yet?" She seemed to feel that she was outwitted and that the Eby stupidity had prevailed again. But I was filled with gratitude toward kindhearted Uncle Christian. May the Lord bless him for his generosity.

Young Benj was detailed to keep the records and do the necessary ciphering. A first installment of pounds equal to twenty thousand dollars was pledged against the debt, with the rest to be paid off the next year. The women promised to sew bags to hold the silver coins being taken to Beasley.

By common consent, the honor of being the agent of the new company they formed fell to Sam. The meeting closed with a prayer of thanksgiving, and Sam was glowing with happiness. So through all this, the Lord has answered our prayers. The settlement of Mennonites on the Beasley Tract will be saved.

○

13

The Hero Returns

It sounds like things are going to work out for the Brickers and their friends to keep their land, after all," said Steven Petersheim. "What a loss if they had to leave their cabins and barns and the fields they had cleared with such hard work."

"Yes," said Annie. "And just think—there will be room for more of their *Freindschaft* (relatives) and friends to move to Upper Canada with them."

"Well," said Steven, "we'd better get our sleep so we can keep our own farm going."

The next evening they rushed back to the house after chores so they could read more from Beccy's journal.

✍

April 1804—We're on our way to Canada! I'm sitting here on this log to write while Sam goes off to see if he can shoot some wild game for our supper.

First, I'll write a bit about our wedding day. Last Tuesday at the Hammer Creek House, we made our marriage covenant in the presence of the bishop and the entire community. Hannes Eby's wife organized the wedding feast that followed the service, and it certainly was bountiful.

Auntie didn't lift a finger to help. She told me that I would surely live to rue the day, and that she had a presentiment that nothing but misfortune awaited those who were not satisfied with the good things the Lord had provided for them in the land of their fathers.

I just smiled indulgently. What had I to fear anywhere with Sam and Menno, following the Lord's leading? Even in the hour of farewell, I was happy, and I'm sure my face was radiant with joy.

After the wedding feast, the women crowded around me to give me good-bye, mingling words of sympathy with their congratulations. Nothing could dampen my spirits; the future looked so wonderful that I was almost in a trance.

Out in the kitchen the men were trying to persuade Sam to accept a bag of silver, a hundred dollars that they had collected to pay him for his trouble in conveying their money to Richard Beasley. But Sam clasped his hands resolutely behind his back and refused to touch it. The five hundred acres Beasley had promised him was all the recompense he wanted.

"But we want to pay you for acting as agent for our land company," Hannes Eby persisted.

"Well, then, give me a cow," Sam said, remembering the cow he owed his brother, John.

"Give him two," cried Uncle Christian, "the best ones we have. He needs to start with good stock."

And so it came about that two sleek Jerseys were tied to the back of the *Weggeli* (buggy), one for us and one for Johns, to replace the one that died on the way from muddy York to the head of Lake Ontario.

Our *Weggeli* is a light, two-wheeled buggy, constructed to convey the money to Canada. The women made two hundred small linen sacks, each able to carry a hundred silver dollars. These were filled with coins and packed into the hold of the *Weggeli*. I was to ride on Menno's back. They provided another horse to pull the *Weggeli* with Sam, the money, and my little *Aussteuer* (trousseau) chest. We would put up a little tent at night.

Also on horseback, John and Jacob Erb, two sturdy single fellows, trailed along like guards, to make sure that we were safe in transporting so much money. They planned to stake claims in the Beasley Tract and later return to marry their girlfriends and take them to Upper Canada.

We left on the afternoon of our wedding day. So that's how we have begun our life together and our journey to the home that awaits us in Canada. We have already encountered many difficulties, but we're much too happy to notice them. No matter how dreary the weather or how weary the way, our thoughts are centered on our home in the heart of Upper Canada and on the good news we will be bringing to the Mennonites there.

Sam says that we'll have a housewarming the first evening, with a public showing of our house and me, his Beccy! I think he's aware that he is returning to the tract as a conquering hero.

There's Sam now, coming back with a turkey gobbler he shot, so I must get busy with dressing and roasting it for supper.

✍

May 1804—We reached the Twenty in safety, but we stopped only long enough for me to get acquainted. We opened the lid of the *Weggeli* and showed the hoard of silver that was to bring a great deliverance to the victims of Beasley's treachery. After staying for only one meal, we turned again to the west, then stopped overnight near the head of the lake. The next day we headed northwest through the Beverly Swamp. By now the settlers had laid logs crosswise to make a corduroy road through the worst places.

It was evening when we at last reached the Beasley Tract.

Sam gave the Erb brothers directions to their relatives. He was determined to push on to the house he had built for me, but as we neared John's cabin, he couldn't withstand the impulse to let his brother into his glorious secret.

He pointed out John's place to me from across the Grand River. The house was dark and silent, but by moonlight we could discern two Conestoga wagons standing in front of it.

"*Was in die Welt* (what in the world)?" exclaimed Sam. "We'd better cross the river and investigate."

"They're asleep," I suggested, meaning John and Annie and the little Brickers.

"Yes, they're sleeping," said Sam when he had poked his nose into a wagon and discovered a coop of chickens with their heads under their wings. "There, I've wakened them up. How they do cackle! And pigs are grunting. I don't know what you think, Beccy, but it looks to me a lot like movin'."

He snooped into the other wagon. "They're movin' me too, Beccy. Here's the bureau I made for you, and the chairs, and everything."

My heart sank. This was so different from the homecoming I was expecting.

"Who's there?" John's voice called out.

"It's Sam!" cried Annie. "Sam has come back!"

"And Beccy!" I added joyously.

Both John and Annie came out to welcome us. Before John could clasp Sam's hand, his eyes fell on the unique cart. He stared at it so curiously that Sam laughed.

"What is it, anyhow?" John wondered.

"Ach," Sam replied modestly, "it's *yuscht* a little *Weggeli*."

John gasped: "You didn't . . ."

"Of course I did," said Sam, swelling with importance. "Didn't I say I would? Come on over once and look in." He handed my little *Aussteuer* chest to John to set on the ground, then opened the lid of the money box and told John to thrust his hand into one of the sacks.

But John was cautious and didn't take chances. "First tell me what's inside that queer little wagon box."

"It won't bite," I said, laughing at him.

"But it's hard and round," added Sam, creating an

86

atmosphere of mystery. "Can you guess what it is?"

"It isn't money, is it?" cried Annie. "You don't mean it's the money!"

Then Sam straightened himself up and said dramatically, "Twenty thousand silver dollars. Two hundred sacks, and a hundred dollars in each. Didn't I say I'd fetch it over?"

"Ach, you, Sam!" was all John could reply—but tears were in his eyes, and we all knew how much relief and gratitude he and Annie were feeling.

"You fetched something else along over," I reminded Sam.

Sam bowed before me and said, with mock solemnity, "I went away single and came back double. Beccy is mine now."

I hastened to protest: "I did not mean myself at all. Did you forget that you have a present for John?"

Sam's eyes sparkled in anticipation of another one of his jokes. "Not a present, Brother John. It's more like repaying a debt." Sam untied one of the Jerseys and led her out before his brother's astonished gaze. Even in the pale moonlight, it was evident that this was no scruffy animal. "How's that for your fifteen dollars, John?" He slapped the cow's lean flank. "You can have the best one—that's for your interest. Now we're square."

"No, we're not," said John, clasping Sam's hand and shaking it wholeheartedly. "I can never repay you. None of us ever can. We didn't think you could do it."

Then Sam laid aside his pride and levity and paid a glowing tribute to the folks at Hammer Creek. "It's their money. They have formed a land company, and I am only their trusted agent. If we were to search the world over, no such friends could ever be found as with our own *Freindschaft* (kinfolk) in the Pennsylvania homeland."

At these words, Annie, who had been struggling with her distraught emotions, burst audibly into tears and fled to my bosom for comfort. Sam shook his head: *This* Heemweh *(homesickness)—would she ever get over it? Pity John!*

"Poor Annie," I said, patting the distressed woman on the back. "Do you want to go back so badly?"

"No! No!" cried Annie. "I don't want to go now. It would kill me to go back. I couldn't leave them here—the graves on the hill." She moaned as we moved close to comfort her.

It was Sam's turn to gape, and mine too. "Graves?" he spit out. "Who?"

"Little Johnny. He went with the diphtheria. And the new baby, the other Johnny. He left me only last week, and not a month old," sobbed Annie.

How sad, I thought. *Of course Annie didn't feel to go now.*

Our hearts were filled with tender emotions as we all, late as it was, trudged up to the little Bricker God's acre. Annie led the party and showed us the little garden—the seat, and the tree that they'd planted between the two mounds. It was a nice idea. We talked about the two boys lying there for a while, and then we prayed the Lord's Prayer together before we returned to the house.

That night we slept under a roof—the first time since our marriage. The minute Sam was awake the next morning, he pulled on his clothes, snatched something to eat, let Menno out of the stall, and hurried off to the neighbors. He was going to have a little visit with his old friend, Joseph Sherk, too.

In the afternoon Sam drove me in the Conestoga, with all our belongings, toward our humble cabin. At last we were going home! On the way, we stopped at the Sherks and found that all the *Freindschaft* had gathered there to greet Sam and be introduced to me. Such a handshaking as then ensued!

Old Sam Betzner, always ready with a pleasant remark, told me, "I want to thank you for a new lease on life."

"But it was Sam," I protested. "I didn't do anything."

"Don't you know there's always a woman at the back of everything?" old man Betzner replied, with twinkling eyes. "What did Sam go back to Hammer Creek for?"

"Why, for the money," I replied.

"And not for you?"

I glanced at Sam and saw that he couldn't conceal the fact that he was greatly pleased with this little dialogue. "I was there," I said, "and he took me."

Old Sam laughed merrily. "If you had been *here,* Sam wouldn't have bothered much about Hammer Creek, I guess. There's always a woman at the back of everything."

Then *Grossmammi* (grandmother) Betzner pushed herself

into the foreground and wanted to see the *Weggeli* and the "twenty million dollars."

"Million!" laughed her husband. "You make it big enough. It's twenty thousand."

Grossmammi shrugged her shoulders. "It's all the same to me. At least it means that we don't have to endure a dangerous journey back to Pennsylvania."

We explained that the *Weggeli* and the money was back at John's place for now. Then we continued on our way. A few more miles along the riverbank, and we would be home!

○

14

A Down Payment

"Wow! What drama!" exclaimed Annie Petersheim when they had followed the story this far. "They are about to move into their own home and sleep in their own bed."

"Ah, yes," agreed Steven with a yawn. "And aren't we glad we have our own nest?"

Annie picked up the lamp and led the way to the bedroom, ready for another night' rest, another day's work, and then the evening together, reading more about the Mennonite pioneers in Canada.

It was only a deserted little log cabin in a clearing, amid virgin forest. The door stood open, and there were no blinds at the windows. No smoke curled upward from the chimney, but to me it finally was home, sweet home.

Sam felt that he must make some apology for it as we walked to the door: "It's small, Beccy, after the Hammer Creek House, and small compared to Richard Beasley's mansion."

"Beasley's palace, furnished with other people's money— your money," I sniffed. "Why, Sam, don't you know yet that *things* don't make happiness! It's *people*—you and me."

On impulse, Sam threw his arms about me and kissed me. Then he picked me up, his bride, and carried me through the door into our "mansion." Sam said he had been dreaming of doing this with me.

What fun we had, carrying in the furniture and the *Aussteuer* chest, and arranging everything to suit us. Every time Sam brought in an armload from the Conestoga, he was singing blithely, and I hummed along, an octave higher.

But the next day, already, it looked as though our happy dream was cracking. A little seed of discord had sprouted in our new home: we had our first tiff. Sam had been over at John's place and returned with the *Weggeli* and our cow. As soon as he came into the house, I asked him, "Where do you intend to keep the money?"

"Ach, we might *yuscht* as well let it out in the *Weggeli*."

"Well, I think it ought to be brought into the house and put under the bed, in the *Aussteuer* chest," I said. "It's empty now, since we are using everything that was in it."

Sam resisted, but I persisted and gave him no peace until he went to the barn and carried the money to the house, sack by sack. But he was not gracious in doing so: "What a *dumm* notion!" he said.

"One of them that grows in the Eby *Dummkepp* (dumbheads)?" I flung back at him. "I heard a lot about them back in Pennsylvania already."

That made Same more impatient than ever. Perhaps he wondered if he had married this wife of his to have her poke fun at him. He dropped the nineteenth and twentieth sacks into the chest and closed the lid with a bang. "There!" he said, sinking wearily into a chair. "Does that suit you?"

I tried to explain that I thought it wise to take some precautions, and that I would never sleep at night if that money, which wasn't ours, was out in the barn.

Sam sat there, glowering at me.

I dropped my head on his shoulder and asked, "We aren't going to fight, are we, Sam?"

He pushed me away and said, "It's for you to say whether we fight."

"You mean you are always ready? Ach, Sam, it's the red hair. That always gives temper."

Then I realized what I had done—reminding him of his besetting "thorn" in the spirit. So I quickly poured oil on his wounds by talking about his good points. "But Sam, temper used well also gives you energy, perseverance, and willpower. I love you, red hair, temper, and all, and I will keep loving you as long as we live."

Sam, now mollified, let me run my fingers through his fiery locks. "Will you love me, Beccy, no matter what happens?"

"No matter what happens," I solemnly avowed. "We promised that to each other when we were married."

"It don't give many women like you, Beccy," he replied tenderly, drawing me to a seat on his knee.

Thus the first cloud on the horizon of our wedded life blew away.

In the days that followed, visitors began to pour in from all sides. They had the excuse that they wanted to meet me, but it really was their curiosity about the *Weggeli* and the sacks of money. Each time it was Sam's extreme pleasure to show the sacks and the *Weggeli*. Nothing could ever induce him to sell the *Weggeli*. "If I can leave nothing else to our children, then they should at least inherit my good name and my most valued possession that doesn't breathe—the *Weggeli*."

✍

Summer 1804—Two weeks after we arrived here, Sam decided it was time to close the deal with Beasley. Daniel and

Jacob Erb were to go with him to take the money to Mr. Ridout, the registrar, whom they trusted, and put the whole matter into his hands. But when the day came that they planned to leave, Sam was in the throes of a fever and not able to go along. So he gave over his sacred charge to his assistants and lent his much-prized *Weggeli* for the trip. He gave them directions, encouraged them valuable counsel, and sent them on their way.

Soon Sam was better again, and we were busy and happy, I with my housekeeping and gardening, and Sam with plowing and seeding and a dozen other things, one of which was building the springhouse. He hauled load after load of large stones from the river and started to build a huge trough to hold barrels of bright, sparkling spring water, and a little stone house to cover it. There I could keep the milk and butter.

One day I returned to the cabin after working several hours with Sam. I was surprised to find that someone had entered the cabin during our absence. Everything had been thrown about in great confusion, every box and barrel opened, the bed dismantled, and the top torn off my tree-trunk table. My little *Aussteuer* chest was smashed to kindling. Terrified, I rushed to the door and shouted for Sam.

At once Sam lost his temper. He hopped about like a madman, vowing that he wouldn't sleep until he had found the Indian who had done this mischief. He would level his wigwam to the ground.

"Sam!" I cried. "It's wicked to talk so."

At first Sam didn't listen. He was off in hot pursuit. "Sam!" I hollered after him. "Come back! It wasn't an Indian at all! It was the money they wanted. Ach, Sam, don't be so *dumm!*"

Sam knew there was logic in what I said. He went over to the Betzners in one direction, and then to the Reicherts in the other, but they had seen nobody. He tramped the woods till he was exhausted but found no clue to the mystery. The spirit of revenge burned within him. He declared that he would keep his eyes and ears open, and if he ever found the culprit, he wouldn't rest until the thief had repaid us for the damage.

A few days later the Erbs returned with the *Weggeli*. They had left the money with Mr. Ridout, the registrar, and they showed us the receipt that he had given them for it.

"But where's the deed?" demanded Sam.

The Erbs explained that Beasley could not be located in York, but he would certainly be there in November, when the legislature would be in session. If they would go back then, the matter would be taken care of more fully. After all, this twenty thousand dollars was a down payment, and by late next year our land company has to finish paying for the sixty thousand acres and clear the title deed.

Sam was impatient and really disgusted about the delay. But I am so thankful that the money was no longer here when our house was ransacked. I'm sure now that Beasley's men did it, but I won't let on to Sam. Perhaps he will forget his thoughts of revenge—which don't fit our Mennonite faith, anyhow.

November 1804—At long last, to the relief of the whole community, the sixty thousand acres of Block Two in the Beasley Tract have been signed over by Richard Beasley. The down payment was accepted in accord with the purchase agreement. We have the official papers here, with the condition that we pay the rest of the purchase price within the stated two-year limit from last fall.

Sam is jubilant. He is assured of his five hundred acres at last, on which to carve a larger homestead out of the wilderness. Here we can plan and dream and raise our family, if the Lord blesses us with children. We have so much to be thankful for.

15

To Go or Not to Go

W ell now, tell me what's happening with Sam Bricker and his Beccy," Steven Petersheim said to Annie one evening as they were finishing the barn chores. "You haven't read any of the story to me for some time. Are they fighting with each other in Canada, or are they at peace?"

"Oh, they are at peace with each other but fighting stumps," replied Annie. "Pioneer life is really heavy work, cutting trees, pulling stumps, clearing stones off the fields, and breaking new ground."

"At least they have a solid deal for their land," said Steven, "so they know that their work will improve their own property and not be stolen from them."

"True. The people of the Hammer Creek community really lived out mutual aid by raising that twenty thousand dollars to pay on the mortgage," his wife added.

"I want to read that part again sometime," said Steven. "I bet kindhearted Christian Eby was behind it all along, setting up his son Johannes to make the speech encouraging the land company, and then making the first pledge. How his wife must have scolded him about his *dumm* Eby notions."

Annie had to smile. "You're right. She was outwitted that time. Let's get to the house quickly so I can read aloud to you about what was happening back at Hammer Creek after Sam and Beccy left."

✍

When Sam left his friends at Hammer Creek, he had the confidence and goodwill of all the shareholders of the company they had formed. They saw him heading to Canada with the sacks of silver coins, his bride, and the Erb brothers. But when the 1805 winter was waning and there was still no word of Sam or the money, they began to show signs of worry about the investment.

Stories began to circulate about Sam's character: There was a claim that Sam had sold a chicken from his father's coop and withheld a commission from part of the sale. Another said that while he was under twenty-one, Sam had put his earnings in the family purse only after a forceful reminder of his duty. People were wondering if seeds of iniquity sown in the child had sprouted in the man. The matter, some thought, would be worth investigating.

But at last came the good news of the successful signing of the bargain with Beasley. Then those wild rumors of Sam's youthful "depravity" were contradicted, and the Bricker reputation for honesty was sustained. Dividing Block Two of the Beasley Tract among the shareholders became the one absorbing topic of conversation in the Hammer Creek community.

The Erb brothers had gone to Hammer Creek on horseback and returned by May with a substantial further payment in silver coins, carried in small leather bags tied to the saddles. There was some dickering over the exchange rate, and Daniel Erb did not receive as much credit for the payment as he had expected. By fall 1905 the shareholders had raised the rest of the payment and sent it the Mennonites in the Beasley Tract. The Erb brothers used it to pay off Block Two on schedule. They secured a deed free of any lien or mortgage.

What rejoicing in Upper Canada and in Pennsylvania! The fathers had come into possession of a large spread of land, and the sons were brought face-to-face with what appeared to be the opportunity of a lifetime. Questions were looming among the girls, too. The time was coming when they would have to choose between a John and the privations of Canada on one hand, or a Jacob and the comforts of Pennsylvania on the other.

By mid April 1806, der glee Bench (Benj Eby) had reached a conclusion: he was going to Canada on horseback that very spring to explore the land that his father had acquired. "You can get your *Aussteuer* (trousseau) ready, Mary," he said to the girl of his choice as he sat with her one evening on the front steps of the Brubacher homestead.

Mary cast her eyes down and blushed becomingly. Her silence and suffusion of blushes gave consent. So Benj left at once for Canada, to build a house in readiness for next spring, when he would take Mary along as his bride.

It was quite a different drama when Jacob Brubacher, with much fear and trepidation, took his heart in his hand and offered them both to Lizzie Eby. "How soon will you be ready, Lizzie?" he asked.

The object of his devotion tossed her pretty head. "Never!" she snapped. "If you go there, you can go alone." With this ultimatum, she turned her back full upon him and added, "If you go to Canada, I'll throw you over forever."

That sounded tragic and final. It killed the last lingering hope that Jacob entertained of homesteading in Canada.

Solemnly he answered, "I won't go, Lizzie. I've changed my mind. You mean more to me than all of Canada."

Then Lizzie turned to face Jacob again, all smiles and dimples. "Do I really?" she asked, satisfied.

Everyone knew that Lizzie's mother, Beccy's Aunt Nancy, was really at the bottom of the girl's refusal.

When Mary Brubacher told her mother, Bevy, that she had promised Benj Eby to go with him to Canada in the spring, Bevy was vehemently opposed. "I can't have you trailin' over there to Canada with Benj Eby in a Conestoga," she stormed. "Rogues like Beasley, those Canadians—all of them—are treacherous. Think of Annie Bricker: she nearly died of lonesomeness, and two of her children are buried because there were no doctors to be had."

Scalding tears dropped on Mary's *Aussteuer* as she worked at preparing it. Meanwhile, her mother kept warning her of the thorny path that lay before her if she persisted in this mad idea of going with Benj to Canada. She pestered Mary to find, instead, a young man who would give her a comfortable home in Pennsylvania. Mary wept in silence but continued to ply her busy needle back and forth. She loved Benj and would go with him to the ends of the earth, if necessary.

When Mary's grandparents, *Grossdaadi* and *Grossmammi* Erb, Bevy's own parents, announced that they had made up their minds to go to Canada with Benj and Mary, Bevy was furious.

"But look how old you are!" she argued. "Canada is for young folks."

"Like Benj and Mary?" replied *Grossmammi* with a twinkle in her eye.

"You're seventy years old already," fumed Bevy.

"No, no, Bevy," insisted *Grossdaadi*, "we're seventy years young." He threw his cane into a corner and pranced around like a man half his years.

Quite against her mother's wishes, Mary was married to Benj Eby in the spring, and they joined a company of twelve Conestogas and fifty people headed for Upper Canada. Among them were *Grossdaadi* Erbs and Benj's sister Susie, married to Josiah Schneider. It was by far the largest party that had ever left Lancaster County for Canada, and the honor of leading the procession fell to Benj.

In addition to their supply of provisions, they had in their keeping a well-hooped barrel; in its bottom was packed a thousand silver dollars in sacks of heavy canvas. On his first trip to Canada, Benj had scouted out more land on a tract to the north of Block Two. He had entered into negotiations with the owner for the purchase of land in Block Three, the valley of a charming river that flowed into the Grand. He had named it the Conestoga River, after a creek in Lancaster County.

Benj had told the owner that he would come back the next spring with the price in silver coin and a group of settlers who would transform the forest into a community of smiling farms. And now they were on their way.

The journey was memorable because of the many misfortunes that befell the party. The almanac must have been misinformed about the weather. Although fair skies were predicted, rain fell day after day, causing rivers to swell and overflow their banks. The linen tops of the Conestogas leaked water by the bucketfuls.

The women and children had to walk long distances while the horses scratched and heaved to tug their heavy wagons up the mountains. Then on the steep downgrades, the men had to use all their ingenuity to keep the wagons and teams under control. It was an endurance test for the whole company.

One of Benj's horses took sick, rolled on the ground, and threatened to die. During a game of quoits, one of the young men accidentally struck his brother on the head with a horseshoe. The lad was picked up for dead but in time regained consciousness, only to learn that his panic-stricken brother had fled to the woods. Four days passed before the fugitive could be located and coaxed to return to the company.

The crossing of the Niagara was always undertaken with no little apprehension, and in their crossing—this time near Lake Erie—a near calamity happened. A terrible storm suddenly blew up when they were in midstream and drove one of the wagon-boats off course. It narrowly escaped being caught by the current and dashed to pieces over the Falls.

There was joy without measure when at last they reached the Twenty, and the weary travelers were assured of rest and refreshment among people of their own kind. There they learned that Levi Moyer had recently been ordained bishop by visiting brethren from Berks County—the first bishop of the Mennonite faith in Canada.

On Sunday morning they went along to the meetinghouse, where at least a hundred people were gathered to hear Levi preach. When everybody had been seated and the service was about to begin, little four-year-old Aaron Schneider, son of Susie and Josiah, insisted that he wanted a drink. His mother steered him to the water pail. But he was still restless, so Susie opened her *Windelsack* (satchel) and gave him a cookie.

The cookies kept him contented for a while, but soon he was whining again. "Be still!" commanded Susie in a whisper. But the child broke into a cry that was disturbing the worshipers. The mother opened the *Windelsack* again, and he plunged his hand inside.

"Cookies is all!" he wailed. With burning cheeks, Susie seized the *Windelsack* in one hand and Aaron in the other and hurried out the door.

The cookie box was in the Conestoga on top of a pyramid of boxes. When Susie climbed into the wagon, she was amazed to find everything thrown about topsy-turvy. Clothes, provisions, and tools were all lying helter-skelter.

Benj's wagon was next to hers. Acting on a sudden impulse, she went over and looked into it. There, before her astonished eyes, she saw the mischief maker, his head and shoulders lost in the depths of the money barrel.

Stealthily, Susie climbed into the wagon and pounced upon the thief, secured him by the collar, and shook him with all her might. She forced him to drop a large bag that he had been filling from the money barrel, and helped him turn out his pockets. Then, confident that the fellow had nothing but what belonged to him, she ushered him out of the wagon and pushed him off.

The man jumped from the wagon with a single bound and like a hunted animal raced for the shelter of the nearest woods. Susie knew she must think and act quickly. She decided not to sound an alarm but to replace the money in the barrel, tidy the Conestogas, and consult with Benj and Mary.

After doing that, Susie slipped back into the meetinghouse quietly and gave her brother a slight signal that she needed him outside. Benj came out immediately, and she led him into the yard for a private conversation.

Benj listened to Susie's story, checked the barrel of money, and commended her for being so brave and discreet. Nothing could be gained by circulating a report of the attempted robbery. It would only worry the people, and "what they don't know won't worry them." He resolved to be more watchful over what was entrusted to him in the future.

◯

16

Wrestling an Angel

So, Annie, this story is starting to sound like a multitude of Israelites on their journey to the Promised Land," Steven Petersheim told his wife as they carried the milk to the house after evening chores.

"Yes, and I think God was with the migrating Mennonites, too," she said. "I can hardly wait to read more. Since rain is moving in tonight, we can read a little longer. You won't be able to work in the fields for a few days, anyhow."

Benj and Mary eventually settled into their new home in the Conestoga Valley, which would soon be a thriving colony. In the spring of 1808, both a gristmill and a sawmill were built by the river, just upstream from John and Annie Bricker's place.

One day Mary heard a wagon stop by their house, so she went to the door. Her face lit up with joy when she saw her mother, Bevy, alight from the wagon. She had left her home in God's country, Pennsylvania, to visit them. Mary stood at the door with open arms to greet and welcome her mother. "So you did come after all!" she exclaimed. "It seems too good to be true!"

Bevy had bad news for Benj. His father, old Christian Eby, was no more. He had gradually grown weaker, and then he was gone. It was a terrible blow for Benj, but he bore it bravely. Mary left her chair and went over to stand beside him. She laid a sympathizing hand on his shoulder and was a comfort to him in his bereavement.

It was long past the usual hour for retiring when Benj carried Bevy's trunk into her bedroom. He wished her good night and pleasant dreams. Then he returned to the kitchen, threw himself wearily into the rocker, and dropped his head upon his chest. He had been sitting there lost in thought for some time when Bevy returned. In her hand she held a parcel wrapped in newspapers and tied securely with a cord.

"It's yours, Benj," she said, thrusting the package into his hand. "Your brother, Hannes, sent it along for you." Benj waited until Bevy had gone to bed and then took the parcel reverently in his hands, undid the wrappings, and discovered the contents.

There was—as he had expected—his father's Bible! Its corners were crumpled and its pages thumb-marked, but to Benj it was a sacred treasure. Did it not contain all the promises that had been his father's stay through all the ups and downs of life? Had he not seen his father's tears fall upon the open pages while the old man prayed for his loved ones before the Throne of Grace?

And was Benjamin, the least of his sons, ever forgotten? Oh, No! More than for all the others, Christian's prayers had ascended for der glee Bench, that he might be kept from evil and grow up to be a blessing to the world.

Overcome with reverence and holy memories, Benj buried his face in his hands. His heart was melted into an infinite tenderness. Tears filled his eyes and dropped upon the already-tearstained pages. What a heart of love his father had! How it must have yearned, as Jacob's of old, over his son Benjamin. Time had turned back twenty years in its flight and made him a child again, "just for tonight"—the happy child he used to be in his father's home at Hammer Creek.

His wife opened the door, stole to his side, and laid her hand upon his head. Then, without a word, Mary went back to bed and let him alone with his thoughts.

Mary! Benj could not remember the time when she did not sympathize with his troubles, this sweetheart of his life.

A piece of paper fell from the table and fluttered to the floor. Benj stooped to pick it up. His father's will! Benj and Susie were to share his Canadian lands, but that was not all. Attached to the bottom of the document was a codicil written by his father's own hand, his last will and testament, and the only one in all the world who could execute it was Benj himself.

"My Bible to Benjamin, with the prayer that he use it to preach the gospel in Canada."

Yielding to an overwhelming impulse to escape somewhere, anywhere, Benj jumped up, opened the door, and slipped out into the night. He looked up into the dazzling dome of the heavens. Then he knew that, go where he would, he could never outrun those myriads of twinkling stars that seemed to search his very soul—"like the eyes of God," as his father used to say.

"But I'm not going to be a preacher." He looked up into the galaxies of the heavens and said so.

Silently the stars twinkled on while Benj protested, now strongly, now weakly. A terrible warfare was going on within his soul. Hour after hour, the battle waged unceasingly, indecisively. But with the first blush of morning light, Benj was ready to fall upon his knees in utter exhaustion. He looked up into the heavens and cried with the outcast Hagar of old, "You, God, you see me."

Then Benj realized that like Jacob of old, he had wrestled

with an angel until daybreak. Humbly he claimed the patriarch's blessing. Then and there was vouchsafed to him a wonderful vision. He saw the Canada of the future, a land rich in resources and teeming with population. The wilderness had blossomed into a garden where once an impenetrable cedar swamp had been. Ah! What a task was his, to lay well the foundation of Christian citizenship in this new land of promise.

With a new aspect on life, Benj returned to Mary's side and announced that his father's prayers had prevailed. He was "willing to offer himself on the altar of the Christian ministry if God and the church wanted him."

Mary was overjoyed. "I've known for quite a while that you were called to preach, and that you would never be truly happy till you gave yourself up. I have been with you in spirit every hour of this past night, and I sensed the moment of your decision. My one anxiety was that perhaps I was unwittingly standing between you and your duty. I thought maybe I was a stumbling block to you, Benj," she confessed.

"A stumbling block!" cried Benj. "Why, Mary, you're my stepping-stone, and I mean that with all my heart. All that is good and lovely and true and sweet—so much and more—is what my Mary means to be."

In due time the church confirmed his call through nominations for a minister, and then the lot, to determine God's choice. When the Sunday came for Benj to give his first sermon, services were held at Old Sam Betzners. People came from miles around to hear him preach, and the house was packed to the doors. And such a sermon it was!

Not even his brother Peter, the bishop, had ever been known to preach like that. It was as if both preacher and people had turned their backs forever on the mundane things of life and had taken a pilgrimage to some lofty mountaintop of religious experience, and there to enjoy a perpetual love feast. They wanted to build a tabernacle and stay there with Moses and Elijah—and Benj Eby. People crowded around him afterward and told him how his words had moved them.

"It was the Lord," replied Benj quietly, refusing to be elated by their praises. "He told me what to say."

A month later, Benj and Mary's first baby was born, a boy

with a pair of lusty lungs. Grandma Bevy was there to welcome him. "We'll call him Isaac, after *Grossdaadi* Brubacher," she said. Much as Benj had hoped to call him Christian, after his own father, he let Mary have her way.

Bevy stayed for quite a while in Canada. "Now that I am a grandmother," she said, "it will never do for me to travel home on horseback." But Benj and Mary knew the real reason: she had come to like it in Canada, the land she had once so fiercely opposed. It was God's country, too.

🖂

Summer 1811 (in Beccy's journal)—Seven happy years have passed since we moved into our humble home here in the Canadian wilds. Sam has been felling trees, clearing more land for farming, and often as I go about my work, I can hear the chop, chop, chop sound of his axe, and the sound of his rich, baritone voice as he sings blithely while swinging it.

Sam's grudge against Richard Beasley has been all but forgotten, I hope. If it ever resurfaces, I hope I am there beside him, coaxing him to put it all into God's hands and to forgive.

Mary and Benj Eby have built a house just across the river from us. Mary teasingly said, "I hope Benj won't be running over to see Sam every morning before breakfast. He's still Benj's hero, same as he always was."

Benj says that the new tract upriver is another Conestoga stream as in Lancaster County, Pennsylvania—a rich, fertile region drained by a river meandering through country so scenic that its beauty alone could justify its existence. He predicts that before long this tract will be the home of a great population, and the beautiful river will water the cattle of many farms.

The Parliament at York decided, several years ago, to encourage the settlement of the Beasley Tract by improving the road through the Beverly Swamp. Great swaths of trees were cut down, the stumps removed from the roadbed, and trunks of the felled trees were laid across the pathway for long stretches and covered with clods of earth. Thus thirty miles of corduroy roads were made, which was a great improvement.

As a result, on the border of the cedar swamp there sprang up, in the months that followed, a colony of Ebys. Sam called it

Ebytown, and the name stuck. My brother, Daniel Eby, and cousin Amos Eby, and many others are here, and so it seems more like God's country to us now than Pennsylvania.

Our own family is growing, too. The recent addition of Baby Sophie makes three: Mary, Peter, and the baby, redheads all. I am happy with Sam and the children, and I know I shall not live to rue the day I hitched up with Sam and his temper, in spite of Bevy Brubacher's prediction long ago.

As Benj said, "If it wasn't for Sam, we'd all be sittin' back in Pennsylvania yet. It was really smart for him to fetch those twenty thousand dollars over." Well, smart or no, I know I'll always love him and will stick by him no matter what happens.

Baby Sophie is crying. Even though little Mary is rocking the cradle, that won't quiet her anymore, so I'll lay this aside.

17

Sam's Outburst

Ah, Steven, doesn't Benj's ordination remind you of when you were made preacher here at Willowcreek? That was a heavy experience for us, but God blessed you in that role."

"Yes, Annie, I thought of that, too. I know what it is to wrestle with God's angel and then humble myself to do as God calls. But then, you're such a help and encouragement to me all the time."

"That's just how I like to hear you talk, Steven! Come on to bed. Tomorrow's another day and, come evening, another chapter, but not from Beccy's journal this time."

☜

Toward the end of July 1912, Little Aaron Schneider created a sensation in the community by becoming alarming ill. This was the same boy who five years earlier had disturbed the meeting at the Twenty with his cries for more cookies. Now his cries of pain made everyone fear that the time had come for Little Aaron to leave them.

Just what ailed the child, nobody knew. He seemed to be suffering from a mixture of diseases, exhibiting all the complaints listed in the almanac and a few others that the medicine makers had failed to mention. Down the little patient's throat had been poured quarts of homemade remedies that the neighbors had brewed from native herbs for his benefit. He had been sweated and starved, rubbed and charmed. As the community saw it, all that was humanly possible had been done. The child's life was now in God's hands.

In these anxious days, only a malicious person might have hinted that the little sufferer's *nixnutzich* (mischievous) ways might have brought such a terrible sickness upon himself. Why, only two weeks earlier, the little fellow had ruined a good set of harness while trying to satisfy a budding faculty for invention. And the previous summer, he had secretly sucked as many as ten eggs in the barn, when they were selling at six cents a dozen. These and other pranks were blotted out of the book of their remembrance. Little Aaron's "sins" of innocence were covered.

The time had come to speak only of the boy's virtues, the qualities that would entitle him to a place in the angel band in heaven. His father told how industrious he had been, helping with the chores night and morning. "He was a good boy, not at all destructive or quarrelsome, like others of his age—the best son an undeserving father ever had."

But his mother kept thinking about how she was going to miss him, and her eyes filled with tears. She folded her hands in resignation over the top of her abdomen, and said with Job of old: "The Lord gives and the Lord takes away; blessed be the name of the Lord."

Sam and Beccy Bricker had always been quite fond of Little

Aaron. He used to visit them every day on his way home from school, and the little Brickers eagerly looked forward to his coming. It seemed as if he almost belonged to the Bricker family. And how Little Aaron was sick and would likely never come again, and they all were sad.

"I made some chicken noodle soup for him," said Beccy one day when Sam brought word home that Susie and Josiah had despaired of his life. "Little Aaron was always great for noodles."

"Noodles!" grunted Sam. "He can't eat noodles now."

"And why not?" asked Beccy. "Noodle soup is good for whatever you've got." She poured into a pail a quart of this panacea for all the ailments of humanity and held it out to Sam. "Take it over to him once. Tell Susie I'll come by tomorrow."

Sam wasn't pleased about the errand, but he obediently put on his hat and rode over to the Schneiders with the noodles. Little Aaron was still alive but hovering between this world and the next. "He don't want to go," Susie said.

Sam presented the noodles Beccy had sent and then followed Susie into the bedroom. The sick child lay upon what everyone feared was his deathbed. In the farthest corner of the room was the bed, and somewhere on top of it was Little Aaron, elevated about halfway to the ceiling and almost invisible.

The bed was a great four-poster with a network of ropes supporting a huge straw tick, overlaid by a billowing tick of feathers. On all the little patient was lying, covered by various handmade quilts of marvelous design, and protected by a dark drapery from drafts and the eyes of the curious.

Susie approached the bed on tiptoe and quietly drew the curtain back. The child was asleep, and she motioned Sam to come and see him. There lay the little fellow, white and haggard almost beyond recognition, a mere skeleton of his former self.

"Does he look natural?" asked Susie in a funereal whisper.

Sam shook his head.

The child moved, turned slowly onto his side, and opened his eyes dazedly.

"Aaron, it's Sam Bricker," said his mother. "He fetched some noodles along over from Beccy. You like noodles, I know. Do you feel for some now?"

But Little Aaron turned his face impatiently to the wall. "I want water, cold water," he mumbled weakly. "I'm hot all over, and my head aches me so."

Sam rushed to the kitchen and brought in a cup of cold water, but Susie brushed him aside unceremoniously. "Are you crazy? The child must be kept hot for fear of a chill." She took the precaution at this moment to tuck a piece of flannel around his neck, lest a cold draft should reach him from the open door.

"Sometimes he gets wild," whispered the distressed mother, pulling the valance again to its usual place and preparing to leave the room. "I often wonder if he's goin' out of his head."

"I'm sure he will," replied Sam, "if you don't give him more air. That's what he needs—air and water."

At this moment a startled cry resounded through the room. Susie and Sam turned again to the bed. Aaron had jerked the curtain aside and now sat bolt upright on the feather tick, with an avalanche of heavy quilts tumbling to the floor. His eyes were sparkling with excitement and fixed on some unseen object in a far corner of the room. With his little white finger, he pointed to a creature of his fancy. "Ketch him, Mom," he cried.

The mother heaved a sigh and stooped to pick up the quilts.

"Give him water!" suggested Sam. "Cool him off!"

But Susie paid him no heed. Gently but firmly, she tried to make the child lie down.

Still Aaron stared fixedly into the corner and shrieked in his delirium. "He's stealin', Mom! He's at the cookies! Ketch him! Quick!"

A great tear fell from Susie's face and splashed on Little Aaron's flushed cheek. The child looked up questioningly. The delirium was gone, and the little body fell back languidly among the feathers. Susie tucked in the quilts securely and pulled the curtains closed once more. She motioned Sam from the room.

"All the time he thinks somebody is stealin'," explained the troubled mother in the kitchen.

"Funny," replied Sam, pulling his whiskers. "Did he see somebody stealin' once?"

"Only that time at the Twenty," said Susie.

"At the Twenty?" exclaimed Sam, pricking up his ears.

The cat was out of the bag. There was nothing for Susie to

do but to relate, in part at least, the story that she and Benj had decided to keep to themselves. She explained that Aaron had been with her when she caught a man rummaging in Benj's Conestoga and reaching into the barrel. It must have made a wonderful impression on the child's mind for him to remember it so vividly five years later.

Sam Bricker got up and paced the floor. His face was dark and foreboding, though Susie in her excitement did not notice. "What did he want—that man?" he demanded to know. "Surely not cookies!"

"The money for Block Three," replied Susie. "Benj had it deep in the barrel."

Sam fairly jumped. "He didn't get none, did he?"

"Not a dollar!" Susie was glad to inform him. "I ketched him and threw him out!"

"What was he like, Susie, this thief?"

At that moment Susie had her first hint of danger, but she did not know what it was or how to avert it. She described the fellow as well as she could. "He was a little man, not a sturdy Mennonite farmer."

Suddenly Sam pounded his fist upon the table with such force that Susie bounced off her chair. "It's him!" he roared.

"Who?" cried Susie in great distress. She saw a black cloud of danger looming up, ready to break over her head.

"Beasley! That scoundrel! That rogue! That thief! He was at our place, too!"

"At your place, Sam? You must be dreamin'."

"I was, but I've *yuscht* wakened up."

"But when was he at your place, Sam?"

"When he smashed Beccy's chest. Now I'll smash him!"

Then Sam was gone. Like a madman, he mounted his horse and rode away. Susie ran to the door and begged him to return for the pail that Beccy had sent with the noodles, but he did not hear. He had no ears for anything but what that devilish temper of his was urging him to do. Sam had no patience even with Menno, though he was straining every muscle to do Sam's bidding.

Utterly bewildered, Susie went back to the kitchen, sat down at the table, and buried her face in her hands. She was still there when Josiah came in and asked, "What's the matter with Sam Bricker? He rode away like a lunatic."

Josiah didn't know what the fuss was about. He thought the matter with Beasley had been settled years ago.

"So it was," replied Susie, "but Sam thinks Beasley tried to steal from Benj at the Twenty."

Since Josiah had never heard the story, Susie had to tell it to him in detail. He was puzzled. "Beasley tried to steal perhaps, but did he get the money? No. Sam ought to be glad instead of mad."

"Ach, Josiah, you are a *Dummkopp* (dumbhead), too, for all you ain't an Eby," returned Susie. "Can't you see how Sam feels? But then you didn't have any trouble with Beasley like Sam did. And he didn't come in here either and smash our things like he did Beccy's chest, her *Aussteuer* chest, no less, all she had in the world."

Josiah had no patience with either Sam Bricker or his logic. "What proof does Sam have," he wanted to know, "that it was Beasley who played the thief in either case? And if it was Beasley, what restitution can be demanded when nothing has been lost? Is a man to have his head smashed because he is suspected of having smashed a trunk years ago? Sam Bricker is nothing but a hothead. There's no knowing where that wild temper of his will lead him yet."

Susie either could not or would not follow her husband's argument. "I can't help but feel for Sam," she kept repeating, "and for Beccy."

Josiah offered her no consolation: "Well, it's all your fault. Why in the world did you have to tell him all you know? Maybe it will learn you a lesson."

Susie said no more. But all night long as she sat at Aaron's bedside, she thought about Sam Bricker. Mingled with her prayers for the recovery of her child were silent but fervent petitions that the man might be given grace and power to withstand this onset of his besetting sin.

◗

18

Gloom

As Steven and Annie Petersheim were eating supper, Steven said, "I can see why Sam would be furious about Beasley trying to steal and cheat them, and smashing Beccy's *Aussteuer* chest yet, too."

"Yes, I agree," said Annie. "But how does he know for sure it was Beasley rummaging in his house and in the Conestoga at the Twenty? Anyhow, I don't think others should blame his temper on his red hair. I have seen red-haired people who were usually calm and steady."

"So have I," said Steven. "And the apostle Paul calls

us to self-control and thinking about things that are noble. That is better than mulling over hurts until we get ourselves worked up."

"Spoken like a true preacher," his wife replied. "Now let's do those chores so we can find out what happens next. Beccy is sure to be worried about where Sam is and what he is doing in his rage. I wonder if he will compromise his Christian confession of being a peacemaker and loving the enemy."

"I wonder that, too," Steven said. "And yet, it is also important to speak the truth to evildoers and call them to repentance and fairness— but in a respectful way."

It was amazing how quickly they did the chores and came back to the house for more of Beccy's journal.

✍

August 1812—Sam is gone, and now I am here alone with the babies. I am afraid that the news of Sam's furious outburst of temper and of his leaving to seek revenge has already spread like wildfire throughout the whole community. There is no excuse for his conduct. It was foolish, extreme, and sinful. Ah, Sam, Sam! What could you have been thinking. The Lord will punish the wrongdoers in his own good time and way. He doesn't need your puny help.

I have been crying my heart out ever since I found out that Sam had left on his crusade. I have always feared for his temper but had hoped that, with me at his side, we could manage his pouts. If only he had come to me first instead of running off to the cruel world. I would have reasoned with him and persuaded him to let it go.

It was from Josiah Schneider that I first learned the truth. He came to return the pail that I had sent over with noodles, and to see if, perchance, Sam might have returned to his senses and come home. Josiah was sorry to tell me what had happened, and then he left me sobbing at the kitchen table.

The next morning Susie came over, her eyes red from tears and sleeplessness, and folded me to her breast, both of us weeping. She was utterly penitent. "If only I had thought—it never entered my *dumm* head that the thief might have been Beasley, or that he might have been the one who ransacked your cabin that day and smashed your *Aussteuer* chest."

"I always felt sure that it was Beasley, but I kept my hunch away from Sam. If only I had been at his side when the crisis came."

"I fervently wish that I had told you first," Susie said.

And if only she had, oh, how I wish it.

"You always were a smart woman, Beccy," she added.

Ach, she needn't flatter me so, but I can't help but wish that she had not told Sam.

Oh, Sam, where are you now? I know him well enough to realize that if he starts something, he won't stop until it's finished—a good quality in its proper place.

Susie tried to cheer me with hopeful reassurances: "Sam won't stay long away from you, Beccy. He's always saying, 'It don't give many women like my Beccy.'"

But, oh, how I fear for Sam's temper.

People have been so kind since I am alone. One by one, the neighbor women have come to mingle their tears with mine and to bring comforting messages. But I have felt so deserted and dejected.

I can't understand why Benj doesn't come or at least send some word of sympathy. Mary has been here and wept with me, but she said nothing of Benj's feelings. Such friends as Benj and Sam have always been—from earliest childhood Benj has idolized Sam. Now, in the day of trouble, does he have not even a word of consolation to offer? I can't help but feel a little hurt about it and a little neglected, too. Maybe he feels too bad to come.

Oh, Sam, how could you have let us down so?

✍

Two weeks later—Tonight after I'd tucked Mary, Peter, and little Sophie into their beds, I went outside, alone with my thoughts, sitting on the doorstep in the glorious twilight of the late summer. Thoughts too deep for utterance surged through my throbbing breast, and a great tear splashed on my folded hands.

Just then I became aware of someone stealing silently up the path, and he sank down on the step beside me. It was Benj.

"It's hard, Beccy," he said with deep emotion. "You know how I feel for you—for us all. Sam . . . my hero—" His voice broke, and he too was shedding tears.

There was a lengthy pause, and then Benj spoke again. "I have to do it, Beccy. It's in the *Ordnung* (church rules)."

Oh, what a pang shot through me after I caught his meaning. "You aren't going to . . ." I couldn't say the terrible words.

Gently Benj did say it: "He's set back from communion, excommunicated. I had to. We can't have him as a member with actions of revenge. It is one thing to have a passing thought of revenge, but we need to overcome temptation, with God's help, and not run around to do vengeance, which is the Lord's."

My eyes were blinded with tears, and I dropped my chin upon my heaving breast, the tears overflowing and coursing down my cheeks.

Benj felt my extreme sorrow. He laid a hand upon my shoulder, quoted a few verses from Scripture, and then stole away as silently as he had come. I'm sure he was glad enough that his part of the ordeal was over, but he knew that I was struggling.

It's just another bitter ingredient added to my cup of woe— Sam's excommunication. He's now under the ban because he has allowed the devil to lead him outside of God's will. He has separated himself from Christ and his church, and unless he repents heartily of his wickedness, he must remain outside.

Oh, Sam, Sam! Little Aaron Schneider is recovering, but we have lost you. My heart is so heavy, and yet I must gather courage for the children's sake. Harvesttime is approaching, and with Sam not here this year, I must take down the scythe and go into the fields to cut the ripened grain, bind it into sheaves, and garner it into the barn.

I'm sure the neighbors will help. Already the men have repeatedly come to offer assistance, but as long as I can and have the strength, I will try to do both Sam's work and my own. The time might come when I can't keep up anymore, and then I will call upon their aid and surely be grateful.

〇

Annie Petersheim settled herself on the Boston rocker the next evening, to read aloud to Steven more of Beccy Bricker's story. It had been hard to put down last night. She felt so sorry for Beccy and wondered what would happen next. Would Sam ever return?

As a fellow preacher, Steven was feeling for Benj in needing to deliver such a difficult message to Beccy. But he understood how important proper housekeeping was for the church fellowship.

Annie began to read more of the story aloud.

Beccy Bricker was worried about the time when she would not be able to handle everything alone anymore. Suddenly and unexpectedly, that time came, and a terrible day it was. Afterward, she could do nothing but wail.

The last sheaf had been gathered in. The brave little woman had just begun the threshing as well as she could, flailing grain on the barn floor, when a terrible scourge broke over the Bricker homestead. It left her homeless, hopeless, and penniless, at the mercy of the community.

It was one of those relentless forest fires that every now and then would swoop down upon the early settlers when they least expected it. The fire would consume everything in its track and leave nothing but a heap of black ruin. It came so suddenly that Beccy did not see it until it literally knocked at her door.

Frantically, she seized Baby Sophie and carried her, cradle and all, to the springhouse. Mary and Peter shrieked with terror and ran behind, clutching at their mother's skirts. Beccy shoved them all into the springhouse, on the cold stone floor, and threw a pail of water on the outside of the heavy wooden door, which alone stood between her helpless little ones and certain death.

The barn! Could she reach it? She must! She could hear the cow bellowing in agony, the horses neighing in alarm, the hens cackling with excitement. Beccy saw flames shoot from the barn roof and the smoke curl from the vents. The hay and sheaves of grain were starting to burn.

The *Weggeli!* Sam's most treasured possession! She saw it

as in a vision, not with physical eyes. Not a moment now did she stop. Throwing her apron about her shoulders, she rushed to the burning barn, opened the door, and rescued the *Weggeli* from the very teeth of the fiery demon. With one hand on either shaft, she dragged it to the wide door of the springhouse. Turning it on its side, she tugged at it with the help of Peter and Mary until she got it safely inside.

Then she closed the door upon the flames, gathered her children into her arms, listened, prayed, and sang a lullaby to calm them.

Presently the roar and tumult of the flames passed by and echoed in the distance. Her children were safe. As brands plucked from the burning, they had escaped with their lives.

A terrible scene of desolation greeted Beccy when she opened the door of the springhouse. A few charred pillars stood where the barn had been. A few frightened hens with singed feathers had managed to flee from the scene of horror and now cackled in frantic protest. The workhorses and Sam's Jersey cow, trapped in their stalls, had died a horrible death.

Nothing was left of the harvest but a mass of smoldering grain and hay, and a cloud of dense, black smoke. The house, blessedly, had come through the furnace of fire with some remnant of its identity. It could yet be saved, Beccy thought, though great tongues of fire still leaped out through holes in the roof, and smoke belched from the windows.

Trembling with stress, Beccy carried a bucket of water to the kitchen door and tried to enter. But a volley of smoke and a blast of heat met her there and drove her back, temporarily blinded and half-suffocated, to her refuge in the springhouse.

"What is it, Mom?" asked Peter, whose eyes were open as wide as saucers with wonder.

Mary, two years older, knew, but she could not explain. She realized that it was her duty to keep Baby Sophie asleep to the terrors of a cruel world.

Utterly dejected and hopeless, Beccy prostrated herself before the little cradle and sobbed as if her heart would break. It was the one piece of furniture that remained to her of her once-happy home—the little cradle that Sam had made.

Scarcely knowing what to do, Mary ceased rocking and

stuck her thumb into her mouth. She went to her mother's side, bent down, and whispered into her ear: "Don't cry, Mommy. You've got us yet."

"Of course I have," cried Beccy, gathering her darlings about her.

They heard voices outside. The neighbors had come and were calling: "Beccy! Beccy!"

"Here she is!" shouted Peter, rushing to the door. Benj Eby was there, and Josiah Schneider, and Beccy's own brother, Daniel. Soon a great crowd of friends and relatives had gathered from far and near.

"Don't cry, Beccy," said Daniel. "We'll make it good, won't we, Benj?"

"We certainly will," replied Benj. "We'll have a building bee, and before you know it, Beccy, you'll have a new house and barn."

"I'll fetch Sam's cow over," said John Bricker. "We never call her anything but Sam's cow anyway."

Tears of gratitude flowed down Beccy's cheeks as she tried to express her thanks. "The good Lord put it into your hearts," she said. "He knows I can't help myself now."

The men worked hard, often leaving work that should have been done at home in order to help Beccy. By the end of November, they had restored the Bricker buildings. With donations from her friends, Beccy was able to furnish her new home almost as well as the ruined one that Sam had made. One by one, neighbors quietly dropped by with contributions until she had two horses, a few pigs, some hens, enough hay and grain for the winter, and so on.

But no matter how kind her friends might be, life was not the same. There was always an aching void. Beccy's very soul cried out for Sam. Sam! But all she heard, all she would ever hear, she feared, was a dismal echo.

One morning when she was going to the barn as usual to do the chores, she saw Menno, as if an apparition, standing at the stable door with only a halter about his neck. Instantly her hearted bounded for joy. Sam! Sam was back! But the *Schimmel* had no rider. Sam was nowhere to be seen.

Anxiously she hurried toward the stable. It was actually

Menno. He saw her coming and ran to meet her. He lowered his head for her embrace, frisked his tail for joy, but whinnied for sorrow. He was asking the same question as she: "Where is Sam?"

Beccy could tell at a glance that it had been many a long day since Menno had been with Sam. The hair was worn off his hide where heavy harness had rubbed. His mouth was sore and his feet poorly shod. It was clear that Menno had served some hard master. Gently she caressed the tangled mane, and then led him into a stall in the barn.

Glad as Beccy was to see Menno, his coming emptied her heart of all hope of Sam's return. Nothing in the world could have persuaded Sam to part with Menno—nothing he could control, that is. And what was there that Sam could not control? His temper. His death! Sam was dead! "He must've went," Beccy reported to others.

Toward the end of March, there was a little rift in the dark clouds over Beccy when a new member came to join the family circle. This was a bouncing boy with eyes as blue as the skies of heaven and hair as red and as curly as his father's.

"Too bad Beccy had to have him yet," said Annie Bricker aside to other women who had come to see the new arrival. "I'm sure she's has it hard enough without another *Boppeli* yet."

"Too bad," they all agreed.

"But she don't think so, not her," continued Annie. "What do you think she wants to call him yet? Sam!"

"Sam?"

"Yes, Sam!"

Susie Schneider thought she could understand how Beccy felt about it: "Maybe he'll grow up to be a comfort to her, poor thing. And Beccy needs all the comfort she can get."

But when the excitement was over and the women had gone home, Beccy was alone with her little ones. Gloom again settled down upon the woman, and sorrow that she could not shake off. Loneliness, it seemed, was to be her lot in life.

She could scarcely remember her parents. Christian Eby, who had been both father and mother to her, had taken his journey to that far-off land of no return. And Sam, to whom she had given all her love, had left her in disgrace, without so much as a farewell. Nearly a year had passed since that terrible day. He had gone on the long journey, too, she was sure. But when or how, she would probably never know. And here she was—alone with her babies—always alone.

Poor Beccy almost stuck in the Slough of Despond known as self-pity. She might have fallen hopelessly into it but for her four helpless children, who came to her rescue and pulled her out.

Mary, the oldest, was agitated about something. She pushed the kitchen door open with all the force she could muster and came to the parental court of law to lay her complaint: "Peter, he slapped Sophie right at the nose and made the bleed come." With one hand, Mary tried to drag the young culprit before the judge; and with the other, she led her little, sob-choked, bloody-nosed, toddler sister.

They came upon Beccy at a most inopportune moment, when her tears were giving vent to her feelings. At the sight of their mother in such distress, the children forgot both accusations and excuses. The judge and lawgiver herself was in trouble. Could it be that someone had slapped her? With wondering eyes they stared at Beccy for a moment. Then all three burst into tears and ran and hid their faces and fears in their mother's apron. For them, it was the darkest hour in their lives.

Beccy roused herself. Casting aside her worries, she turned to her children. Tenderly she lifted little Sophie to her lap and wiped her dirty face. She put her arms around Mary and Peter and drew them close to her breast. "You must not quarrel," she said. "The great God who has made you brother and sister wants you to love each other. You must promise not to quarrel and hurt one another anymore."

"We will be good," they promised. Beccy smiled through her tears to hear them make their solemn vows.

The children went back to their play and soon forgot the episode. But the mother's heart was filled with a new joy. Alone in the world? Not Beccy Bricker with three small children clinging to her skirts, and another, the most helpless of all, crying in the cradle. On the spot, she made up her mind to think no more about her troubles. Instead, she would plan and work for her little ones—hers and Sam's.

When suppertime came, Mary brought the dishes and set the table. Never once since Sam had left had she neglected to set a plate for her father. But this evening Beccy said, "Please put it back in the cupboard."

"Ain't he comin' ever?" asked the child, with anxious, questioning eyes. She knew that there was some mystery about the sudden disappearance of the *Daadi,* but just what it was, her young mind had not yet been able to fathom. "Ain't he comin' no more?"

"No," said the mother. "He's went."

"Then we must have his funeral," said Mary, in the matter-of-fact way in which she had heard her elders speak of the last sad rites.

Beccy turned her face away and for a while said nothing. But she determined to be brave: "No, Mary. He's had his funeral already."

"And we didn't go to it?"

"We couldn't, Mary. We didn't know yet when it was. When you are old enough, we will go together and see if we can find his grave. Would you like that, Mary?"

"No!" she cried. "I want my *Daadi.*"

"Ach, Mary, so do I!" Beccy pressed the child to her bosom. "Nobody knows how I want him!"

When evening came, Beccy heard the children lisp their prayers. Then she tucked them into their beds, kissing them all softly and patting their chubby little cheeks. She put the baby into his cradle and rocked him to sleep. But she could not leave her precious baby boy. "Sam, Sam," she cried from the depths of her burdened heart. "Little Sam."

Her heart was full of tender memories and love. Full of happiness, too, the only happiness she would ever know, that of living and working for her helpless little ones. God was very good. He had not left her alone. Who could not be happy with such a family?

After a while she stole quietly from the room and went to the kitchen table. She reached for her mending. Ach, Peter's stocking had a hole in the toe, and another in the heel. Such a boy! But someday he would be a good man, this same Peter, a preacher perhaps, or a teacher. She must train him well so that when his days were over, people would say that the world was better because he had lived in it.

Sophie's little dress was stained with blood. There wasn't a clean one, either. Perhaps she could shorten one of Mary's. Someday both Mary and Sophie would grow up to be useful women, happy wives, she hoped. Here a sigh escaped Beccy, and instantly she coughed to hide it.

Little Sam was the most precious of them all. Here was his little nightgown, handed down from his elders until now it was too old to mend. Well, he would soon outgrow it, and then it would go into the ragbag. And what did the future hold for Little Sam? She intended that he should be just like his father. But he must learn to control his temper and live at peace with all. What better could she wish for him?

Suddenly the little mother found herself enveloped by a pale white light. With a start she looked up and saw that a cloud had passed, and through the window shone the moon in all its glory. "It's full!" she cried, joyfully. For a moment it seemed as though Sam sat by her side beneath the apple tree, with his arm around her. A blissful moment.

But the light in her eyes soon darkened, and another cloud hid the face of the moon. "Silly!" she muttered to herself as she folded up her mending. "The moon don't mean nothing to me now. Ach, Sam, I guess I am *dumm* like all the Ebys!"

◖

19

Sam Down

H ow bad can this get?" asked Annie Petersheim. "One thing after the other has hit poor Beccy. And now she has no husband by her side and four little ones to raise. Ei, yi, yi."

"I want to know what Sam thought he was doing, taking off like that," commented Steven. "I hope the book will tell us what happened to him."

"Yes, I think we might find out tomorrow evening," said Annie. "Steven, I'm so glad *you* didn't run away from *me!*" she teased her husband.

"Ya, well, and Annie, I'm also glad *you* didn't run away from *me*," he joked in return. "Now to bed. Tomorrow's another day."

✍

Meanwhile, Sam Bricker was having the experience of his lifetime. He may have nurtured the most devilish plot against the old enemy, Richard Beasley, but the chance to carry it out always seemed to be thwarted. No doubt kind Providence was intervening.

When Sam reached Coote's Paradise, he was met by an impudent wag who introduced himself as Fred Frid. "Where are you going?" he asked.

"To the head of the lake," Sam replied.

"Say, Dutchie," Fred said, "where did you get that horse?"

"Bought him."

"A wonderful horse. And how much would you take for him?"

Sam's reply was lofty: "He's not for sale."

"Don't blame you at all, Dutchie," said the genial Fred Frid. "Say, I'll give you a night's lodging here. There won't be any accommodations at the head of the lake because it is so late."

So Sam slept that night in the room of the talkative Fred, and stabled his horse as arranged by his new friend, in his uncle's stall. When he awoke in the morning, Fred was gone. Sam rushed to the stable. Menno was gone! The stall was empty except for a big placard: "Thanks for the $15 and the horse that money couldn't buy. Your old friends, Peter Potter and Fred Frid (Peddlers of ideas to people that don't have any of their own)."

Sam was prostrated with grief and rage. The horrid truth flashed upon his mind. Peter Potter and Fred Frid were the same person. Menno, the greatest animal friend he possessed, was in the hands of this contemptible fellow.

With a renewed zest for revenge, Sam pressed on. By the time he had reached the head of the lake and was close to Beasley's mansion, running and stumbling along, he was exhausted. There he collided with an official of such distinction that at his coming, everyone else upon the street stepped aside and saluted. But Sam didn't even see him and accidentally bumped into him.

He was a small man and tottered a bit, though he didn't fall; but it did make him look ridiculous. Sam hastened to apologize, but the aggrieved officer was too furious to listen. He cursed Sam roundly for being a fool, and then strode off with steps that seemed too long for his fat little body.

Sam was too taken aback to do anything but stare. Who was this man? His voice had a ring in it that he seemed to recognize, and in spite of his uniform, his figure looked familiar. Sam had not gotten to see his eyes, which avoided Sam's. But Sam had an impression that he had been not-looked-at in just the same way at some time in his past experience.

"Who was that fellow?" Sam asked one of the amused bystanders.

"Him? Why, the colonel! Colonel Beasley!"

"Little men need big hats," remarked another man, with a cynical smile.

Sam tried to laugh, but the effort sounded weak and hollow. The next minute he was walking up to Beasley's residence and asking the doorman, sporting two rows of large brass buttons, if he might see the colonel.

"He's out" was the gruff reply.

"He *yuscht* came in. I saw him," persisted Sam.

"Take my advice, young man," said the man behind the buttons. "The colonel is out, and I don't know when he's coming back. If you are going to make a fuss about it, there's a nice dark hole in the cellar that I've got orders to run you into."

Poor Sam gasped. He staggered back to the road and threw himself down upon the grass. The spirit of revenge consumed him. If it cost him his life, he was going to pay Beasley back. He would hurl him from his pedestal, expose his treachery, and heap shame and contempt upon his haughty head.

Sam's dogged will urged him on. Mile after mile he trudged, by the power of his quest for revenge. When he reached York, he was dismayed to find that Isaac Brock, the administrator he sought to help him, had gone to the Niagara Peninsula to fortify Upper Canada. It was a great disappointment, but Sam braced himself remarkably well. He made a few fruitless inquiries, then decided that he would not give up his quest. Sam headed for the Niagara Peninsula.

The roads were bad, and Sam's shoes were wearing out. He became so weary of limb and even of life itself that he wished he could lie down by the roadside and cease to be. But still the spirit of revenge possessed him and kept him alive. It grew and nourished him like "a green bay tree" in an arid land (Psalm 37:35).

On one occasion, Sam fell sick and lay down by the roadside to die. But a kind old woman took him into her home and nursed him as well as she knew how. Sam lay unconscious for days at a time, on the no-man's-land between two worlds. He lost all track of time.

His thirst for vengeance made him press on as soon as he was able to walk. The autumn had come, and already the trees were bedecking themselves in the brilliant foliage of the season. The nights were frosty and damp. It was a marvel how Sam, in his weakened physical condition, could endure such extremes of heat and cold as day and night presented.

At last Sam came to the great Niagara River. There he learned that Isaac Brock had been shot in a battle. The friend he thought could help him had died, and so did every lingering hope of revenge within Sam. His shoulders drooped, his chest sank in, and blank despair seized him. He had no more chance of recovering his long-lost Menno, no hope of dislodging the robber Richard Beasley from his seat of power and dignity.

With a broken heart and a conviction that life was no longer worth living, Sam turned again to the west and began to stumble along the road that led toward home and Beccy. He had thought of them both many times during his travels. A deep and relentless shame filled him, and he felt like he could never again face his people on the Beasley Tract. If he could only slink away out of sight, out of existence, somewhere, anywhere, he would never ask anything more of life.

Weary and faint, he sank upon the grass by the roadside and longed for death. That very day it happened that a good Samaritan passed that way, stopped his horse, and came to his relief. Sam opened his wondering eyes and beheld, not the angel of death, but—Levi Moyer!

Levi looked at him and gasped: "You're not—you can't be, Sam Bricker?"

"That's who I used to be" was Sam's reply.

It was the middle of October when the Moyers put Sam between the white sheets of their spare bed and undertook to restore him to his former self. It was a difficult task, for their patient was sick not only in body, but also in mind and spirit. Not a day passed without Rachel preparing some tempting dish, and Levi spent hours at his side. Through the long winter months, they pulled the bed into the kitchen, where it was warmer. But month after month went by, and Sam kept getting weaker and weaker.

"Best let Beccy know," advised Rachel.

"No! No!" pleaded Sam.

"Maybe till spring you'll be well enough to go and tell her yourself," said Rachel hopefully.

But when spring came, Sam's feeble life was still hanging by a thread.

◗

20

My Beccy

Poor Sam," muttered Steven Petersheim. "At least a good Mennonite family is caring for him now. I wonder if he'll pull through."

"Ah, yes," said Annie, "that good Mennonite food and tender loving care can do a lot. I think he might make it yet."

"With God's help," her husband added. "That was such a short chapter. Do we have to stop now?"

And so they read into the night, captivated by the story and hoping that Sam would survive.

One beautiful day in early July, a ragged man might have been seen limping his way up the path that led to Beccy's kitchen. Every few steps he turned and glanced about apprehensively. He stopped when he reached the doorstep, wiped his eyes with his coat sleeve, and noiselessly lifted the latch.

Only the children were in the room. They stopped their play to stare at the intruder.

The man acted strangely, so the children kept watching him wonderingly. He sank into a chair and sobbed like a child. After a while he beckoned Mary to him. "Don't you know me yet?" he asked hungrily.

Mary shrank back, and because she did not know what else to do, she rocked the cradle faster. Peter and Sophie stared hard at the newcomer some more, then scrambled up from the floor and stood, one at either end of the cradle, sucking their thumbs.

Children as they were, they knew that there must be something wrong with the man. He got up from his chair, staggered toward them, but fell into a second chair. All the while he kept his eyes fixed on the cradle and its tiny occupant, who lay kicking and screaming with temper and too much rocking.

"Be still!" warned Mary, rocking with even more vigor.

The stranger looked at Mary, smiled weakly, and asked, "How do you call the *Boppeli*?"

"Sam."

"Sam!" The man's face was radiant with joy. He stumbled over to the cradle, stopped its motion, and knelt before it, kissing Little Sam tenderly on each cheek.

Mary was too surprised to say anything. Even the baby was quiet in amazement.

"Where's your *Mammi*?" asked this strange, presuming man.

"Out in the barn."

Mary was glad enough to see him go, this man who asked so many questions and acted so weirdly. She was not frightened, but she wondered who he was and why he was so sad. She had a feeling that her mother would know better what to do with him.

Out to the barn went the man. It was surprising how quickly

he covered the ground. When he reached the door, he paused and wiped his eyes once more upon his coat sleeve. Then he pushed the door open. Mary, watching from the kitchen window, saw him seize the doorjamb for support and heard him utter a joyful cry.

"Menno!" he gasped.

The *Schimmel* turned his head and neighed. Such a pricking up of ears and frisking of tail and stamping of hooves!

Beccy heard the commotion and came running to see what was the matter.

"Beccy!" cried Sam, rushing to meet her with extended arms.

"Sam! Sam! Is it you? Ach, Sam!"

They were all three together again. Sam stood in the middle with one arm around Beccy and the other about Menno's neck, while tears of regret and joy filled his eyes.

"You don't feel hard against me, Beccy?" he asked as soon as he could command the words. "To think I went away and let you alone—you and Little Sam."

Beccy's head was on Sam's throbbing breast. She could feel his heart pounding. She looked up into his dear, swimming, penitent eyes and said, "I've never been so happy in all my life." Her loneliness and sorrow had only helped her to appreciate this great joy that had so unexpectedly come to her. "Sorrow is for one alone, Sam," she said, "but happiness—"

"Happiness is for two," Sam finished the sentence for her. "I know that, too, Beccy, but I didn't know how to say it."

Then the happy wife led her straying husband back into the bosom of his family. "It's your *Daadi* come back, Mary!" she cried joyfully. "Make the dishes on the table. Come here once, Peter. Don't you know him no more? Ain't Sophie growed, Sam!"

"And the *Boppeli*," said Sam, who couldn't keep his eyes off the little bundle of babyhood that was kicking and crowing in the cradle. "Who does he look like?"

"He's got Sam Bricker wrote all over him," replied Beccy with a laugh, "red hair and all." She knew that was what Sam wanted her to say, and it really was true.

After supper, Beccy pushed Sam into the rocking chair, and

the children crowded around, sitting on his knee and climbing over his back. He was a happy father again, so happy that he quite forgot his physical weakness. "Ach, Beccy," he cried, "this is *yuscht* like old times."

"We'll play horse like we used to do," said Peter, recalling former days and clapping his chubby hands in glee. He knew where the reins were and the stick of wood that they always used as a bit. He pressed them into Sam's hands.

"I want to be a horse, too," cried Mary.

They made a splendid team. Sam tied the cord around his wrist and held the youngest Brickers on his lap; Peter and Mary pranced about, kicking, neighing, and pulling on their bits, like regular thoroughbreds. Sophie decided to be a dog, and she bobbed about the room, running from one side of the team to the other, yelping quite as effectively as Hundli did upon occasion.

"Let the *Boppeli* drive," demanded the children, forgetting for the moment that animals do not use human speech.

So Little Sam's baby fingers clasped the cord, while *Daadi* Sam's great horny ones held it securely. With one accord, the drivers and the horses and even little Hundli joined merrily in a familiar ditty, something between a song and a recitation:

Reite, reite Gäule,
Alle Stunde Meile,
Bis nuff zum alte Blockhaus.
Datt gucke drei Buwe raus.
Eener schpinnt Seide,
Eener wickelt Weide,
Der Dritt macht ee rother Rock
Für mei grosser Zottelbock.

(Ride, ride horses,
A whole hour's time
Up to the old log cabin.
There three boys look out.
One spins silk,
One warps willow,
The third makes one red coat
For my great shaggy ram.)

Such a commotion as there was! The more the baby laughed, the oftener the horses reared up and stamped their feet. And what a bark the funny little dog did have. It was a mercy there wasn't a runaway. They careened all around the room and came back again to where they had started. Then Sam, in the most realistic tone, cried out: "Whoa! Whoa! Why, here we are to home again!"

The romp over, Little Sam was consigned once more to his cradle, and the other children prepared for bed. Beccy heard their prayers as usual, but tonight they insisted that Sam should hear them, too, and help to tuck them into their beds. Having recovered their father, they intended to make use of him.

When Sam and Beccy closed the bedroom door and found themselves alone in the kitchen, a serious conversation ensued.

Sam began it: "I'm not so bad with my temper like I was, Beccy. Levi Moyer learned me a lot."

"Levi Moyer!" exclaimed Beccy. "Was that where you were all the time?"

Then Sam had to give an account of himself. It was a long, sad story, but he had to explain how it happened that he lost his horse and came, after much wandering, to the home of the Moyers. He tried to shorten it, but Beccy insisted upon knowing even the smallest detain of the terrible experience that had aged her Sam ten years in twelve months.

"It was all my temper," Sam told her. "Levi nearly gave me up, but at the end he made me see that I was wrong."

"God doesn't need your help to punish the wicked," said Beccy. "In the Bible, God says he will do it himself."

"That's what Levi told me," agreed Sam. "The Lord says, 'Vengeance is mine. I will repay'" (Romans 12:19).

"And all the time you were runnin' after Beasley and that Fred Frid, they didn't even know how you felt. But you had to suffer, though."

"Yes," said Sam. "Levi Moyer said I hurt myself more than I hurt them. I was very *dumm*, Beccy; I know it now."

Beccy was determined to drive the lesson home. "The Lord must have laughed a lot at you, Sam," she said. "Runnin' all over Canada and tryin' to get people to help you, and never once askin' him."

"And he was the only one who could," added Sam shamefacedly. "That's *yuscht* what Levi was sayin'."

"And when you found Beasley, you didn't even know him. Ach, Sam, it looks to me like the Lord had a hand in that, too."

Sam looked at Beccy earnestly. "To think that I had to go all the way to the Twenty to let Levi Moyer tell me that, when my own Beccy could do it *yuscht* as well. It don't give many women like you, Beccy. It don't give many women like you."

Then Sam wanted to know about the fire, and Beccy gave a graphic description of that terrible visitation. She did not forget to tell how the *Weggeli* was threatened.

Sam listened with bated breath. He could not wait until Beccy got to the end of her story to learn the fate of the historic vehicle. "It didn't burn, Beccy, that *Weggeli*, did it?" he asked.

"No," replied Beccy with laughter in her eyes. "I saved it. I thought I might *yuscht* as well. You might want to sell it sometime."

Sam knew that Beccy was only teasing him. Nevertheless, he made haste to tell her once again that nothing in the world would ever induce him to part with that relic. It was more precious in his eyes than a hundred Conestogas. "First thing in the morning, I am going out to have a look at it again."

They drifted into the news of the community. Beccy reported, "Old Sam Betzner went, and Abraham Gingrich is goin', and George Clemens—"

"He ain't, Beccy, not George Clemens!" gasped Sam.

"Not him," replied Beccy, "but all four *Boppelin*, one followin' in the footsteps of the other. The cholera."

Sam's head dropped upon his chest. "It's hard to understand," he finally muttered. "Four took from George Clemens, and when Sam Bricker comes home, where he should've stayed, what does he find? All safe, and a new *Boppeli* in the bargain. Ach, Beccy, it's more than I deserve. Go and fetch the Good Book once. I must read where it says about the cup runnin' over. I could have written that psalm myself."

Beccy got the Bible and listened with a happy heart while Sam read Psalm 23. When he came to the words "I will dwell in the house of the Lord forever," his little wife's face glowed with joy. But no sooner had he closed the book than all the joy faded from her face in a trice, and an anxious expression took its place.

"What's wrong?" asked Sam, glancing at her.

"Nothing," replied Beccy, smiling blandly. She meant that there was nothing she wanted to tell him just then.

In fact, in that moment of prophetic hope that marked the closing words of the psalm, something had flashed through Beccy's mind: the realization that Sam wasn't going to get a chance to "dwell in the house of the Lord forever." He was set back, banned. The rules called for him to receive a cool reception in every other house on the Beasley Tract.

Beccy had a fertile mind. It did not take her long to evolve a plan to meet the need of the hour. Sam must be received back into the fold. Moreover, he must never know how near he had come to being an outcast among his own people.

Sam was very tired and sleepy. His head had little more than touched the pillow when he fell asleep. Beccy waited until his heavy breathing grew into a hearty snore. Then, quick as a flash, she jumped up, stole noiselessly from the house, and ran out to the barn. She slapped the saddle onto Menno, led him out of the stable, and rode away with speed.

Across the river she traveled, coming at last to Benj Eby's house. All was dark, but she had no compunction about rousing Benj from his sleep to tell him the good news of Sam's return. Her husband had come back, penitent and godly. The devil was no longer enthroned in his heart and life. She entreated Benj to lift the ban and by the next evening to bring the community to welcome the wanderer.

Benj was glad to conspire with her to make Sam's return a matter of general rejoicing. "Expect a great crowd at seven o'clock," he said.

Then Beccy, delighted beyond words with this promise, rode back through the night and crept noiselessly to her place at the side of her sleeping husband.

Sam stirred, put out his hand, and felt for her. "Are you there, Beccy?" he asked.

"Yes," she replied, unable to suppress a smile and glad for the cover of darkness. "Did you think I would run away?"

"No," said Sam, "but I wanted to be sure. It don't give many women like you, Beccy."

The next morning Sam was the most impatient creature imaginable. He seemed to expect that everybody in the neighborhood was going to rush over before breakfast to see him. When the morning was nearly gone and not even brother John had appeared, he did not know what to think of it.

"But," Beccy reminded him, "he doesn't know yet that you are home."

"Then I must go and tell him once," said Sam.

"But we want you here to ourselves for one whole day this year," Beccy urged.

After awhile Sam said, "I'm goin' to take Menno and go over to see George Clemens and tell him how I feel about the cholera taking his young ones."

Beccy was at her wits' end to dissuade him. When she finally succeeded, he began to pace the floor like a lion in a cage.

"As far as I can see, Sam," said Beccy, "you ain't changed much yet for all that."

Sam was heartily ashamed of his conduct. He came and sat down quietly and penitently at Beccy's side.

"Who knows? Maybe we'll have more visitors yet than we have chairs for," his good wife said.

No sooner had they put the children to bed after supper than Hundli began to bark, and a rumbling of wheels was heard.

"Somebody's comin'," cried Sam, springing up excitedly and opening the door.

They all came, and they all came together, after gathering at Benj's place and agreeing to receive the penitent Sam back into fellowship: the Brickers, the Ebys, the Schneiders, the Clemenses, the Betzners, and the Erbs, with a sprinkling of Bechtels, Gingrichs, and Richerts. It was a marvel how they all squeezed into Beccy's little kitchen.

Benj Eby was the spokesman. In the name of the meeting, he welcomed Sam back not only to the bosom of his family and to the circle of his *Freindschaft* (kinfolk), but also to the spiritual brotherhood of the Mennonite faith.

Sam looked so puzzled that Beccy laughed outright and reminded him of her prophecy that they would have more visitors than chairs. At this, everybody looked around to see how the crowd was managing, and they laughed heartily at the makeshift seating.

"But how did you all know I was here?" Sam wanted to know.

"Beccy told us," they answered.

"Beccy!" exclaimed Sam, unable to solve the mystery. "Why, she was at home all the time."

"Except when you were sleepin'," laughed the *mixnutzich* (mischievous) Beccy. "How do you know what all I was doin' then?"

He didn't, of course. But by piecing together the remarks that followed, Sam got the story. "My Beccy is a brave woman, a heroine," he said. He did not try to conceal the fact that he was proud of her beyond bounds.

"She learned it off you, I guess," said Joseph Sherk. "That time you and she fetched the money over."

This reference to Sam's historic journey afforded an opportunity for the host to conduct the party to the barn by lantern light, to see the *Weggeli* again. Once more the marvelous story of their deliverance was reviewed. Sam Bricker was the hero, and Beccy the heroine, both God's servants chosen to deliver his people.

"It was all Sam's doing," Beccy declared. "I just came along."

But Sam didn't agree. "Beccy did her part, too," he said loyally. "She drew me back to Hammer Creek and our friends there and—ach, I don't know right how to say it, but it don't give many women like my Beccy."

○

21

Spring

Annie Petersheim laid the Bricker book aside, yawned, and leaned back in the Boston rocker. "Done at last," she told Steven. "My voice is tired from all this reading to you."

"What a story!" Steven said as he stood and stretched. "I'm relieved that Sam did go back to Beccy and his children, and that the church recognized his repentance and received him back into fellowship."

"Yes, that's for sure," said Annie. "Talk about Eby *Dummkepp* (dumbheads)—it was Sam who was *dumm* there for awhile, running off from Beccy, in search of vengeance. Such a temper! And people thought it came from his red hair."

Steven laughed. "Where it came from doesn't matter. With God's help, we have to deal with what the Lord dishes up to us in our genes. And that's where Sam went wrong. He tried to take vengeance into his own hands instead of trusting God. Anyhow, Sam must be in his grave for 150 years already. Did he really repent and change his ways?"

Annie nodded. "Yes, he came to his senses after a lot of suffering. Poor Beccy! But in the end, it turned out well. Beccy welcomed him back with open arms, and his church brothers and sisters accepted him back into fellowship.

"The last words of the book were 'It don't give many women like my Beccy.' But one thing I can't understand: if Sam thought so much of Beccy, why did he leave her like that without even saying good-bye? It goes to show how strong his thirst for revenge was."

"Ya, well," said Steven, "Sam and Beccy found their way, and we have to find ours, too. Tomorrow night I have to start working on our income tax reports or we may have to escape to Canada ourselves. It's already past our bedtime—"

"Oh, say, I forgot to tell you," Annie interrupted. "There was a letter from your Pennsylvania *Freindschaft* today. Your mother wrote that your sister Susie is able to come to Tennessee and be our *Maad* (maid) this coming summer. She's really looking forward to it. And Dannie wants to be our *Gnecht* (hired man) again, too. That's good news."

"*Wunderbaar* (wonderful)!" chuckled Steven, using Dannie's favorite expression. "We sure will be able to use their help."

"Spring will soon be here," Annie said dreamily. "The birds will be singing, the flowers blooming, and the garden ready for planting before we know it. I can hardly wait.

"So let's get to bed. I have a busy day planned for tomorrow. There's the bread to make, that last rooster to butcher, cookies to bake, and a pile of mending and ironing to do. And in the afternoon I plan to help Vernie make noodles."

"Just that?" teased Steven. "It don't give many women like my Annie."